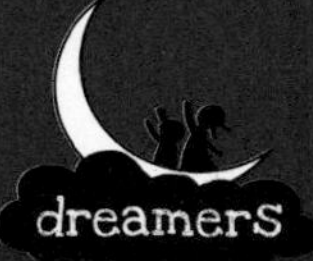

THE BOY WHO BUILT A SECRET GARDEN

This book belongs to

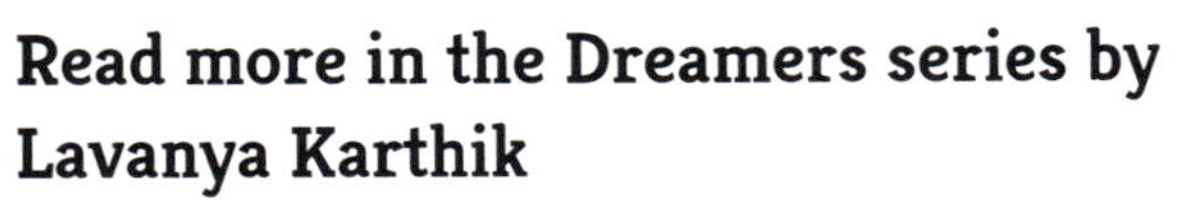

Read more in the Dreamers series by Lavanya Karthik

The Girl Who Loved to Sing: Teejan Bai
The Boy Who Played with Light: Satyajit Ray
The Girl Who Was a Forest: Janaki Ammal
The Boys Who Created Malgudi: R.K. Narayan and R.K. Laxman
The Girl Who Climbed Mountains: Bachendri Pal
The Boy Who Loved Birds: Salim Ali
The Girl Who Loved Words: Mahasweta Devi
The Boy Who Made Magic: P.C. Sorcar
The Girl Who Loved to Run: P.T. Usha
The Boy Who Loved to Fly: J.R.D. Tata

Scan QR code to access the
Penguin Random House India website

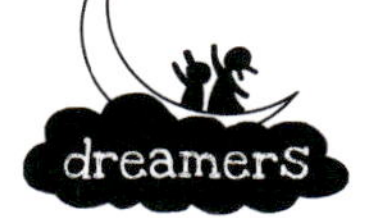

THE BOY WHO BUILT A SECRET GARDEN

NEK CHAND

Written and illustrated by

LAVANYA KARTHIK

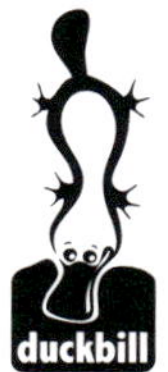

An imprint of Penguin Random House

For you, and the gardens you will build.

DUCKBILL BOOKS

USA | Canada | UK | Ireland | Australia
New Zealand | India | South Africa | China | Singapore

Duckbill Books is part of the Penguin Random House group of companies
whose addresses can be found at global.penguinrandomhouse.com

Published by Penguin Random House India Pvt. Ltd
4th Floor, Capital Tower 1, MG Road,
Gurugram 122 002, Haryana, India

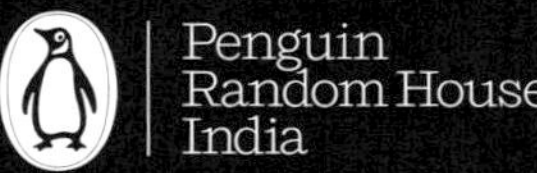

First published in Duckbill Books by
Penguin Random House India 2024

Text and illustrations copyright © Lavanya Karthik 2024

ISBN 9780143464761

Typeset in Georgia by DiTech Publishing Services Pvt. Ltd
Printed at Aarvee Promotions, India

www.penguin.co.in

Before the Rock Garden in Chandigarh became renowned across the world, it was a secret that grew from the memories of one man. His name was Nek Chand Saini, and this is his story.

The city of Chandigarh was meant to be a symbol of a new India, one made of rules and order, straight lines and and hard edges. A city that would never allow a secret garden.

This is its story too.

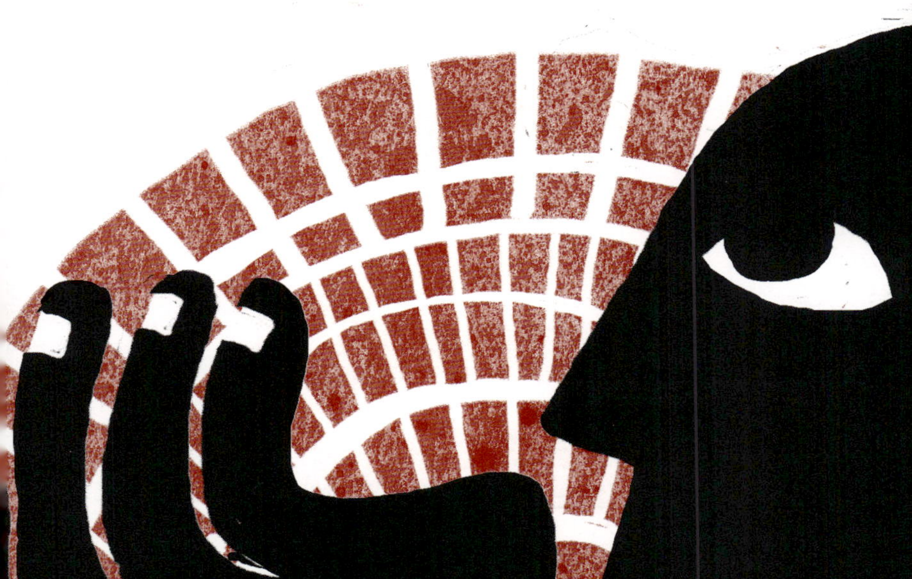

In the village of Barian Kalan in Punjab, in an India still under foreign rule, Nek grows a garden.

It sprouts from unusual things— sticks and stones from the fields, clay from the stream by his house, bits of shattered pots and cups from Ma's kitchen and slivers of bangles his sisters love to wear.

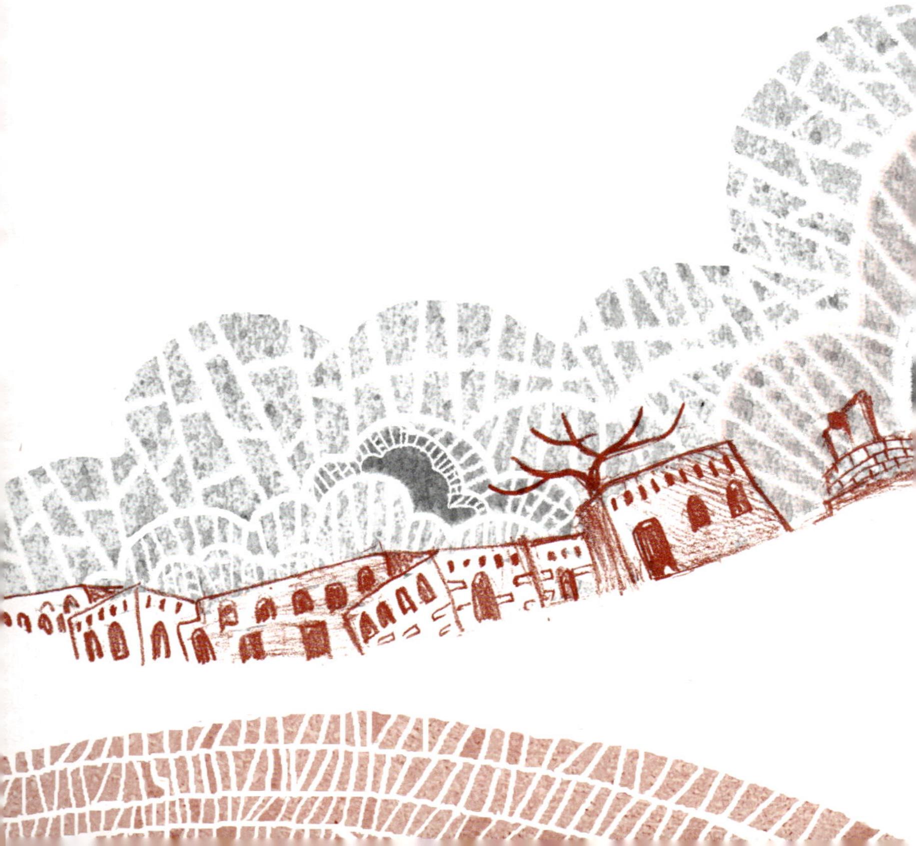

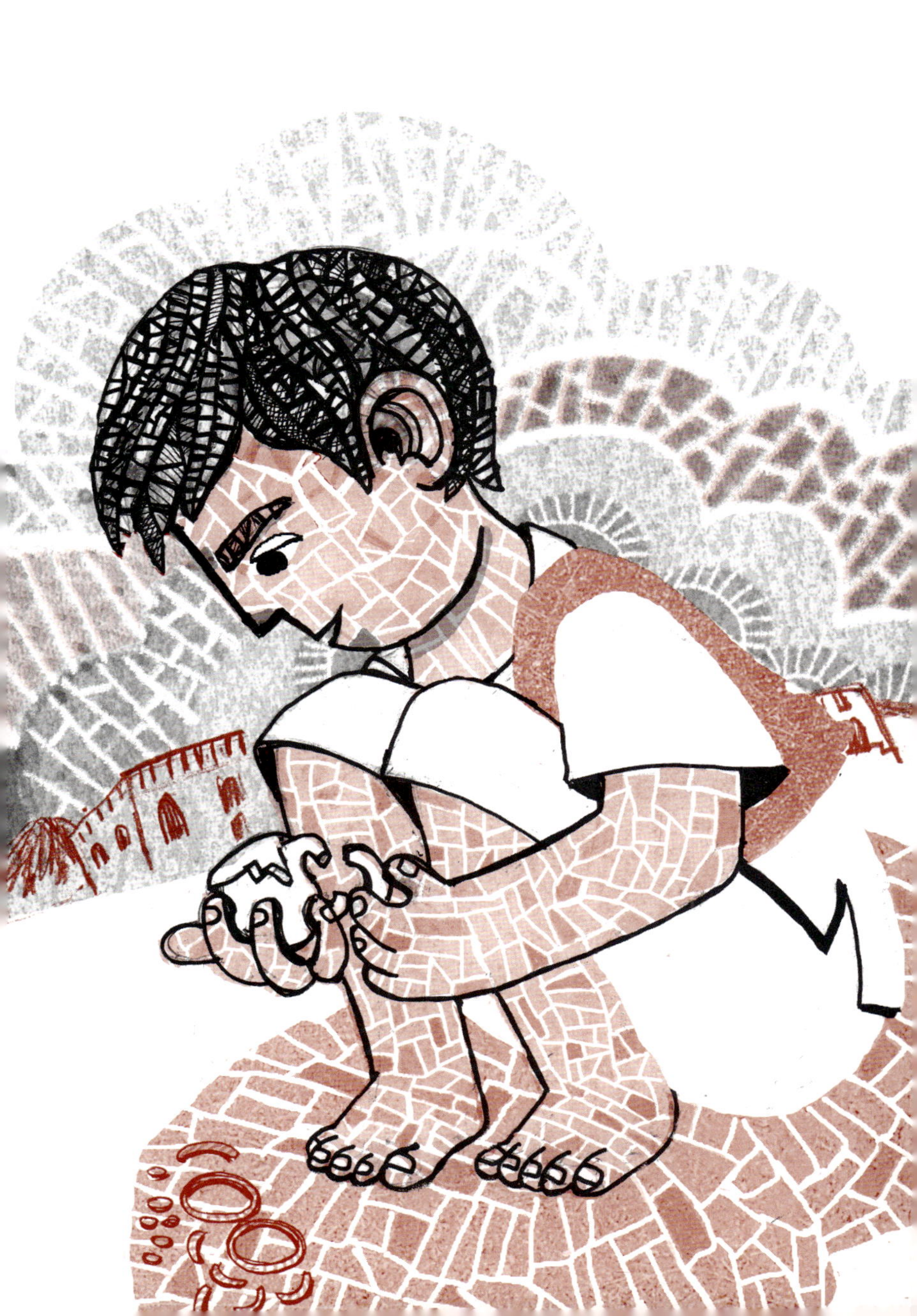

And what grows in this garden?

The kings and queens in his father's stories, the gods of his mother's songs, the monsters from the tales his friends tell in school and the animals he sees in the fields.

Seasons pass. Years flow by. Nek grows, and so does his garden.

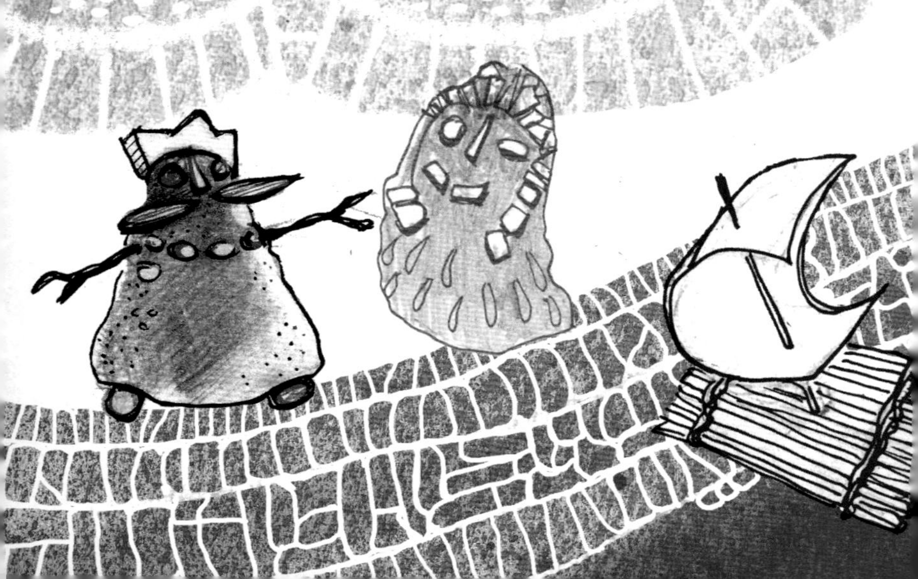

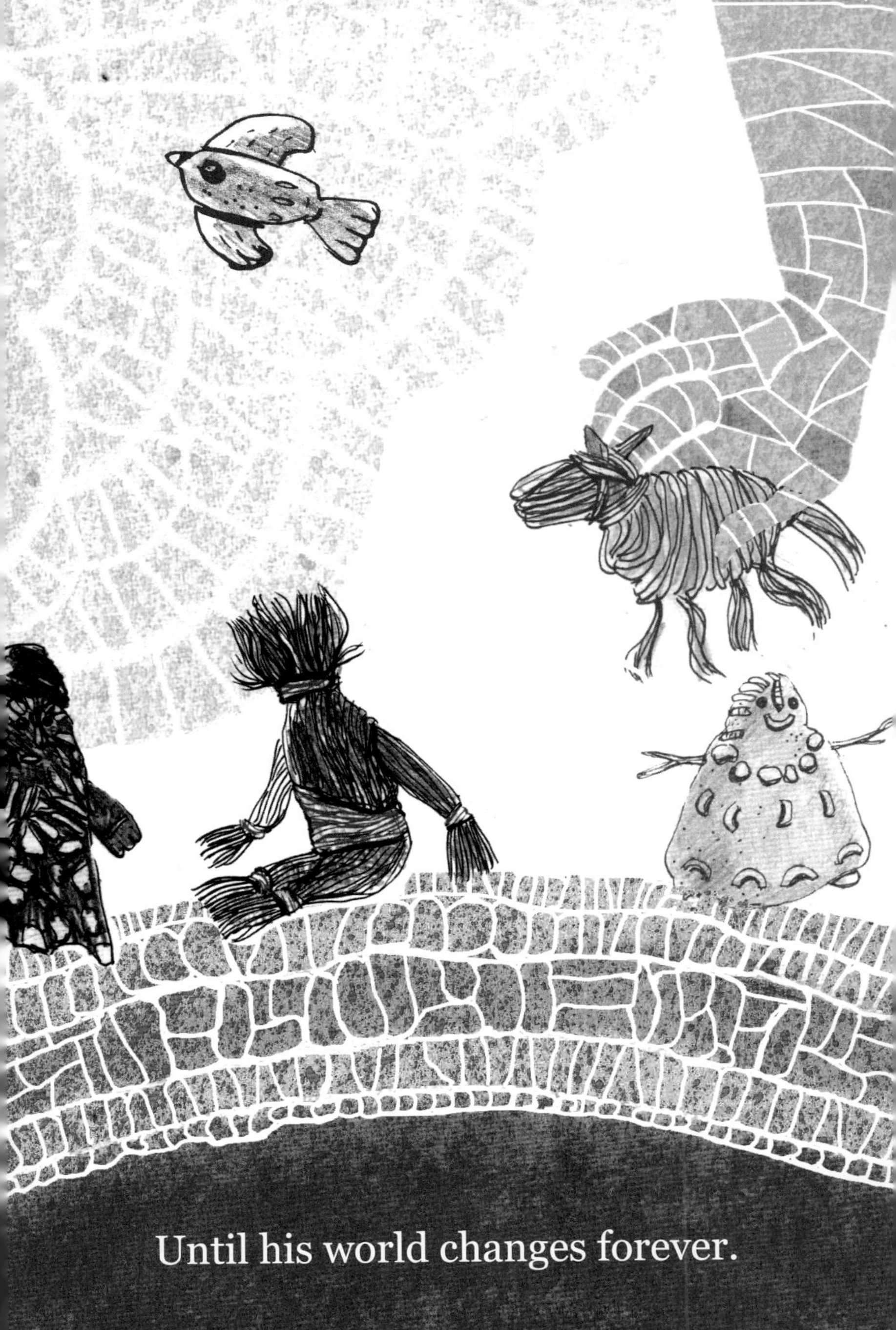

Until his world changes forever.

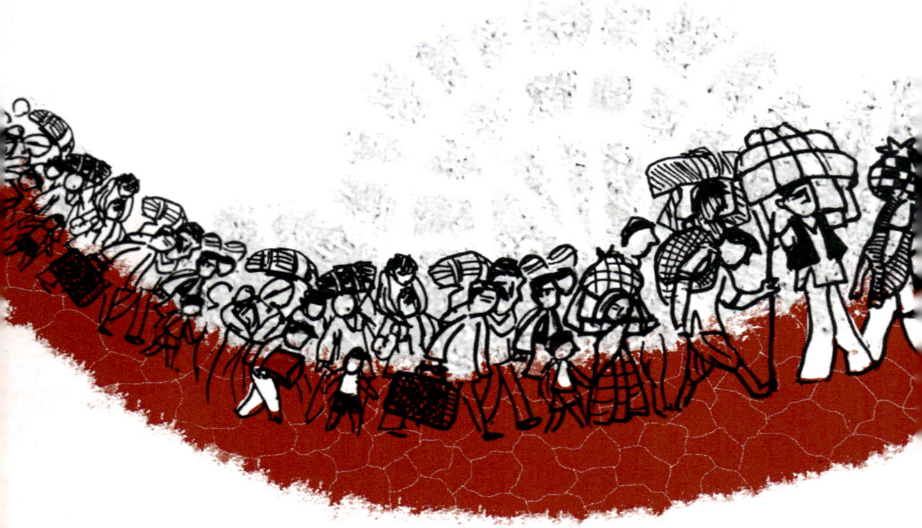

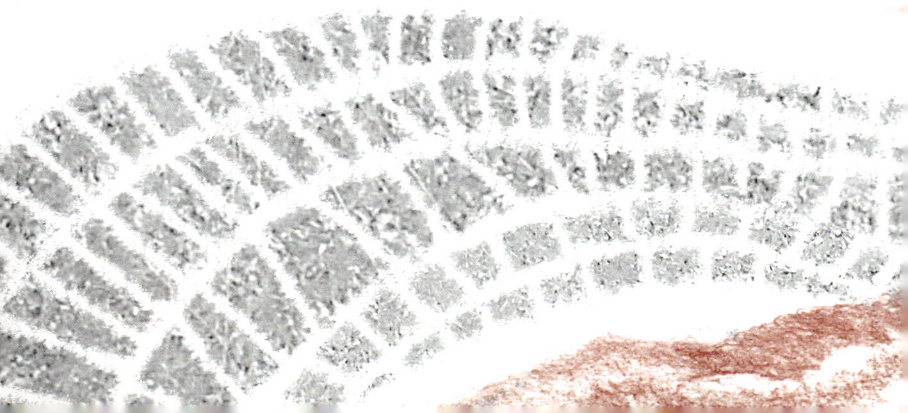

In 1947, Punjab is ripped apart
by partition. New borders spring up,
turning neighbours into strangers
and friends into foes.

Forced to leave their home,
Nek and his family make a long,
dangerous journey to safety.

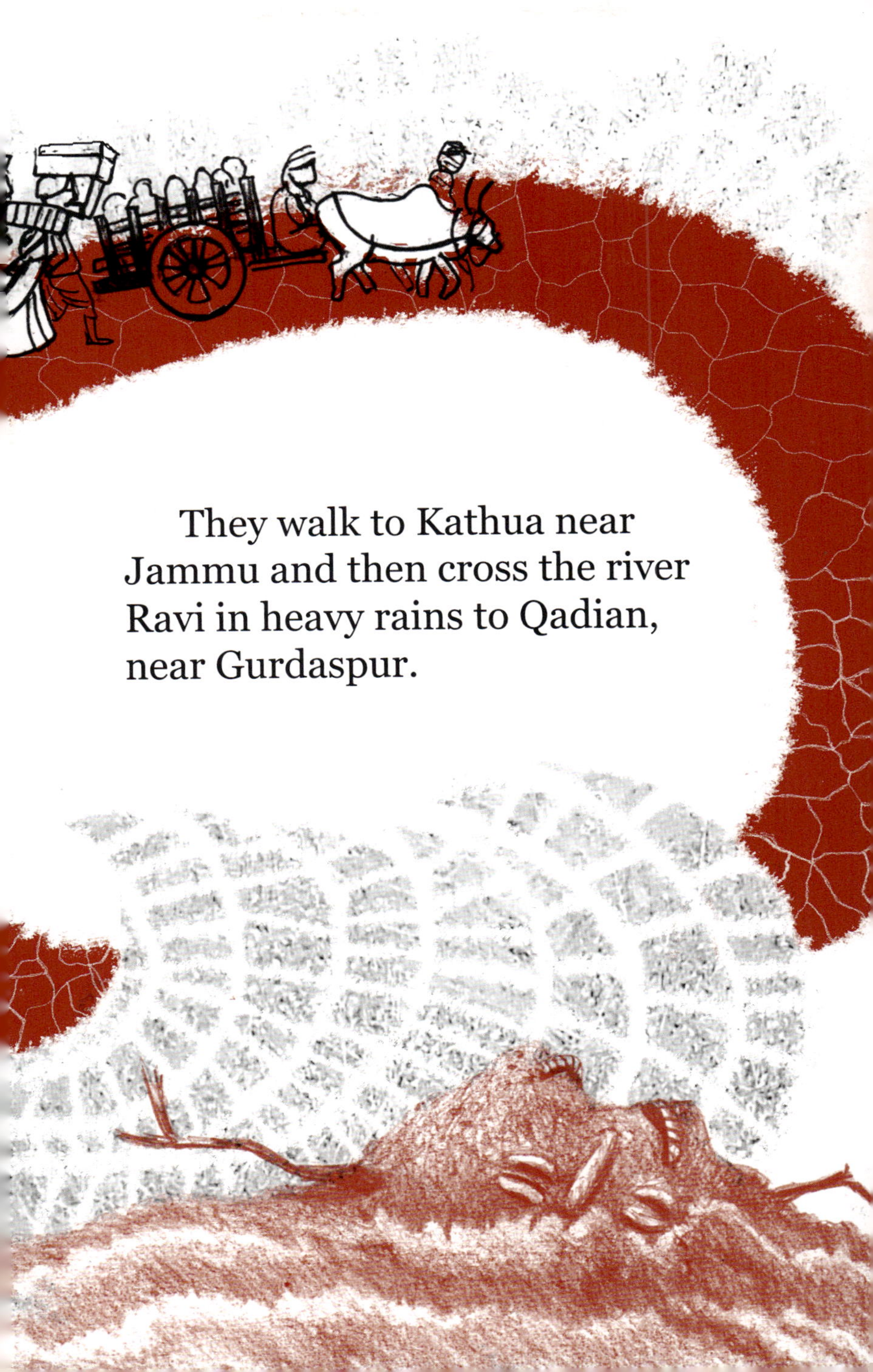

They walk to Kathua near
Jammu and then cross the river
Ravi in heavy rains to Qadian,
near Gurdaspur.

In Qadian, the family begins a new life.

Nek helps rebuild mud huts washed away by the Ravi. He returns to school to finish his education.

His garden becomes a distant memory, like the home he has lost forever.

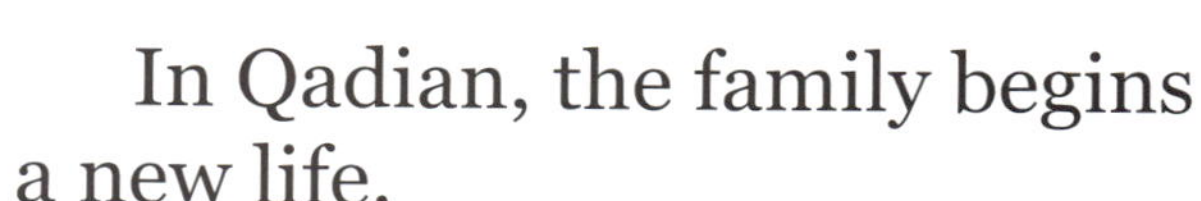

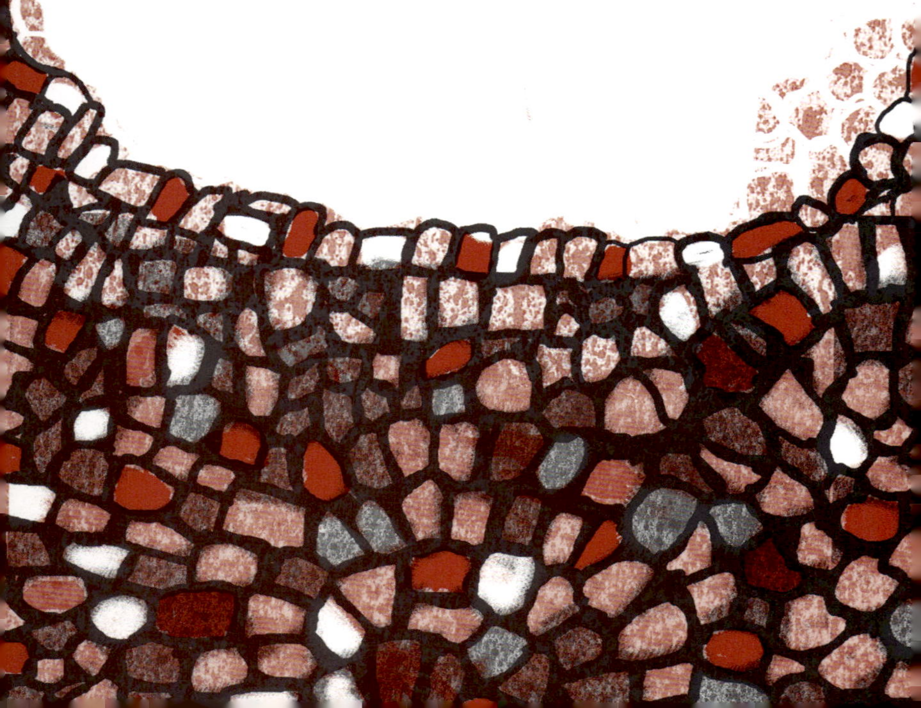

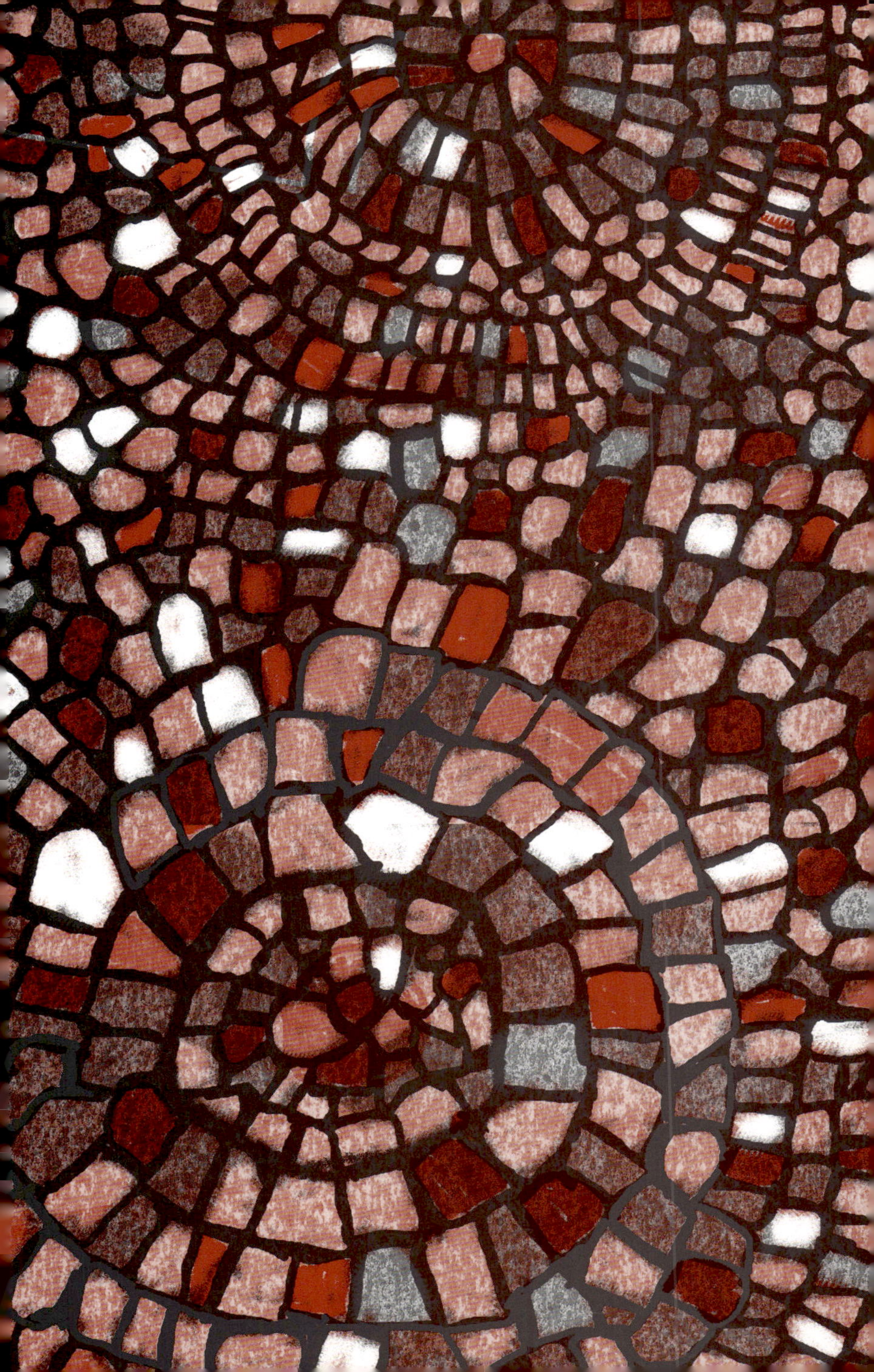

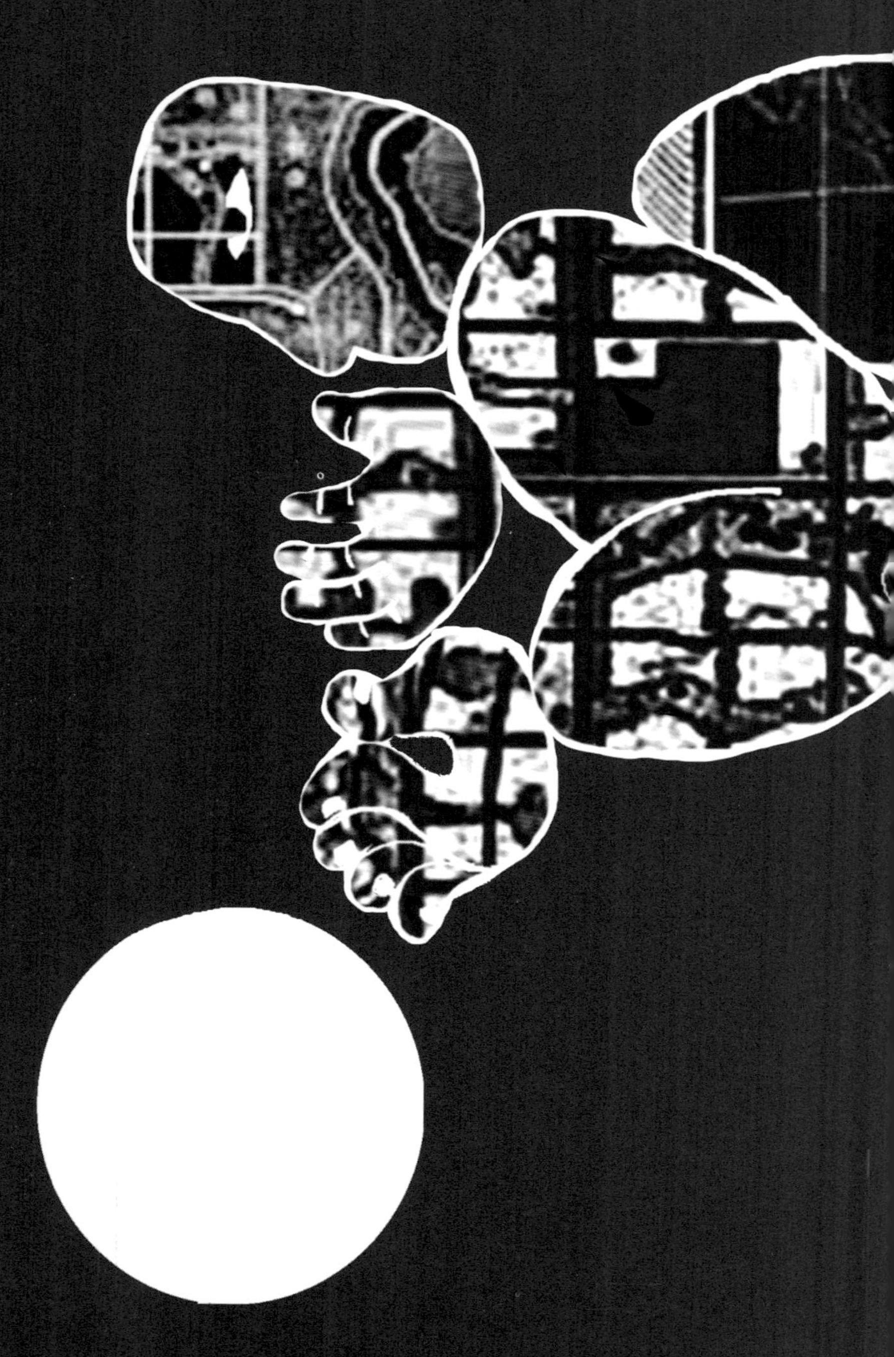

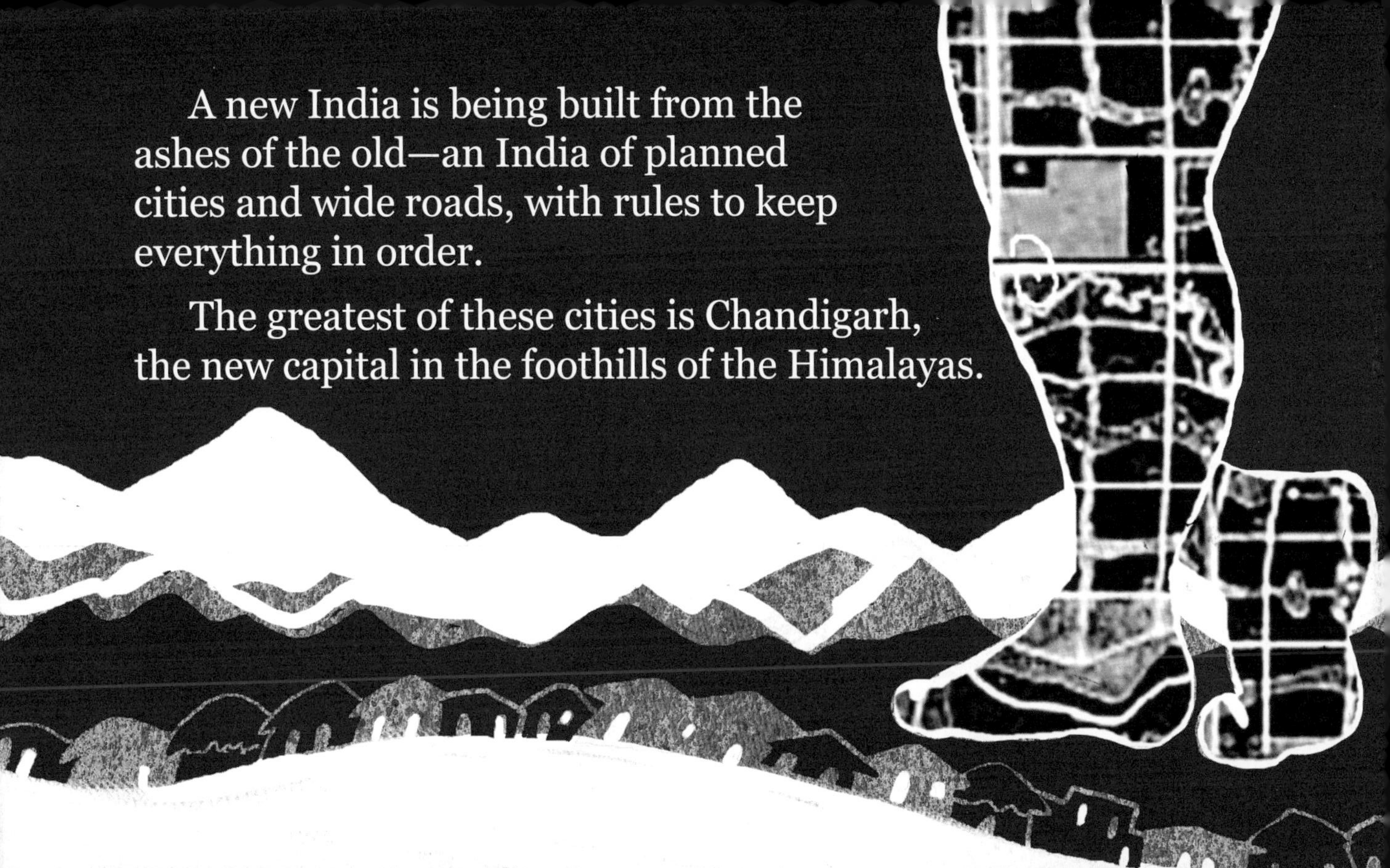

A new India is being built from the ashes of the old—an India of planned cities and wide roads, with rules to keep everything in order.

The greatest of these cities is Chandigarh, the new capital in the foothills of the Himalayas.

Many villages are demolished to make way for the City and its grand roads and offices.

Thousands of people come to the City and begin work on building it. Among them is a young road inspector—Nek.

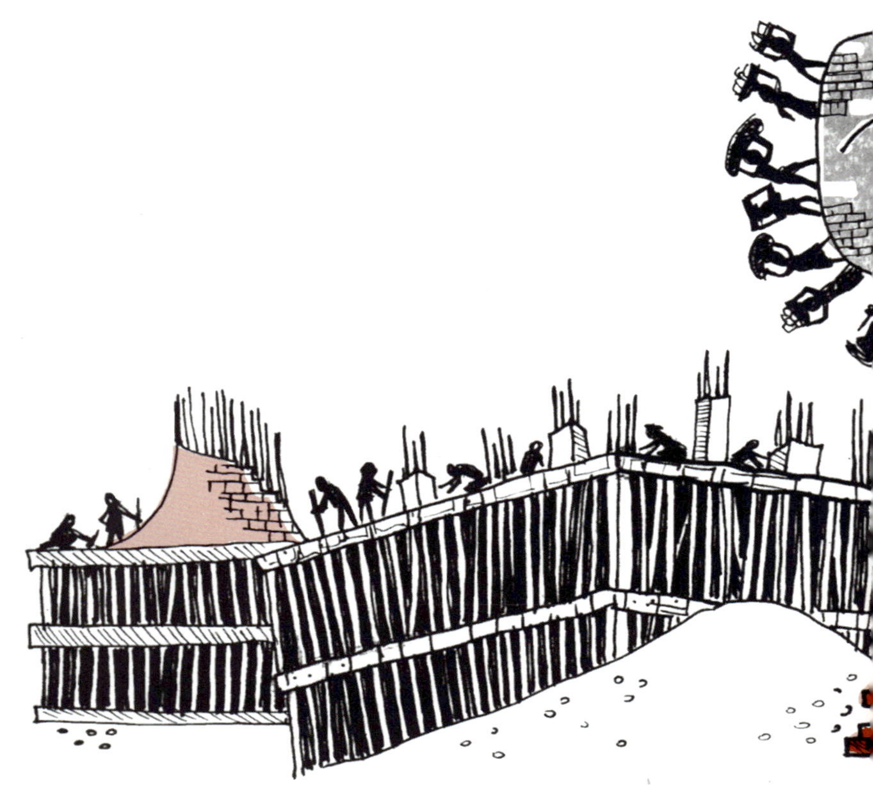

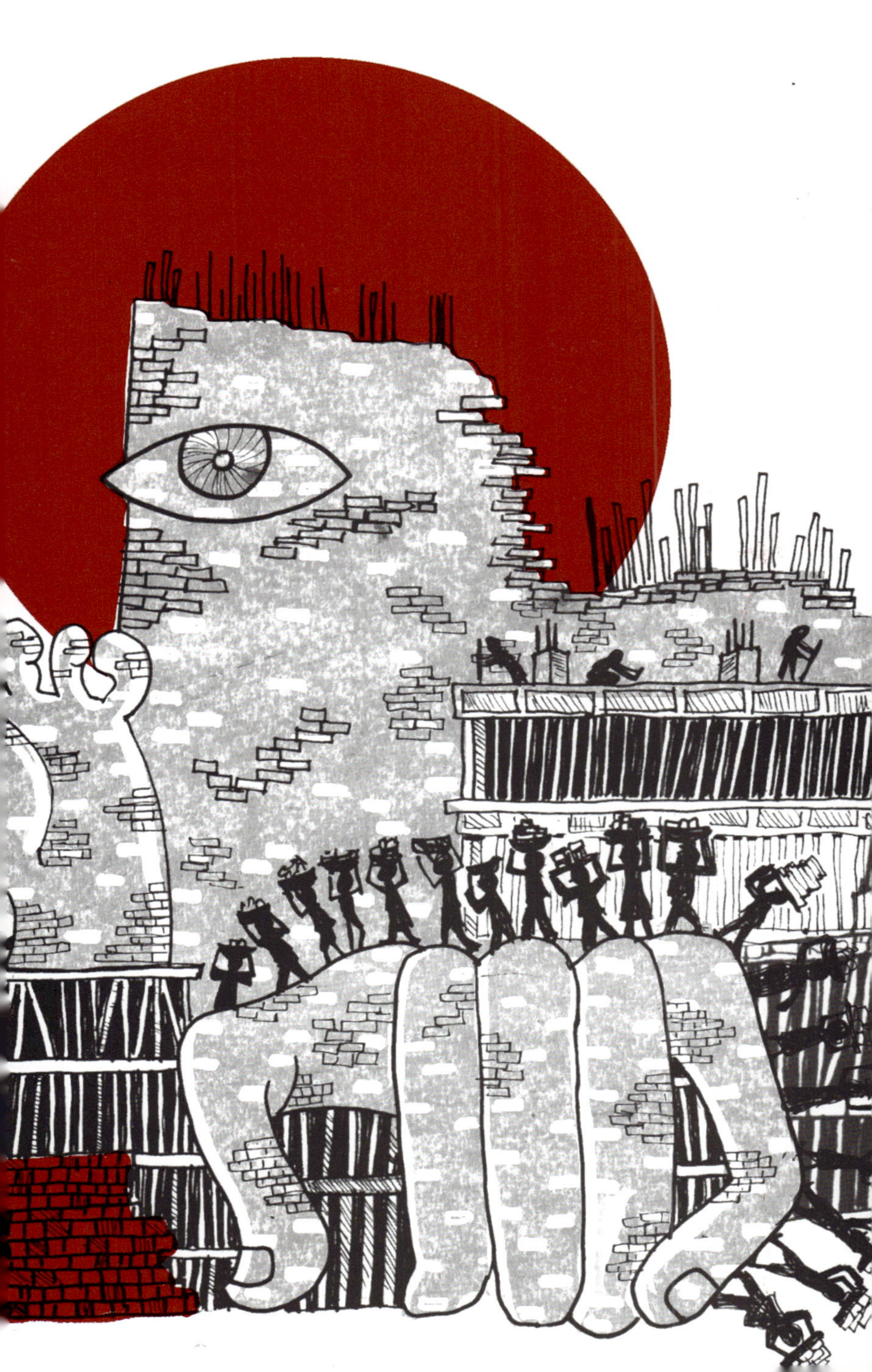

As the City grows, Nek walks
through the remains of the villages.

He sees what the City throws
away.

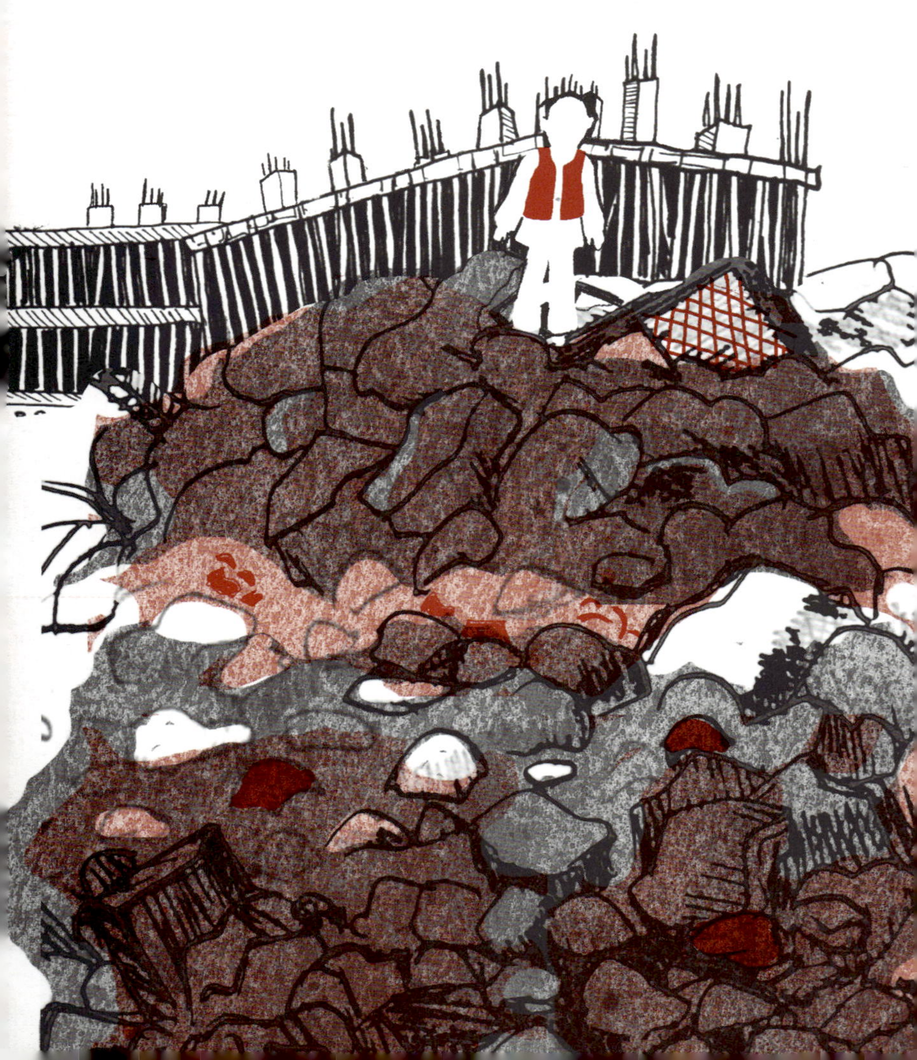

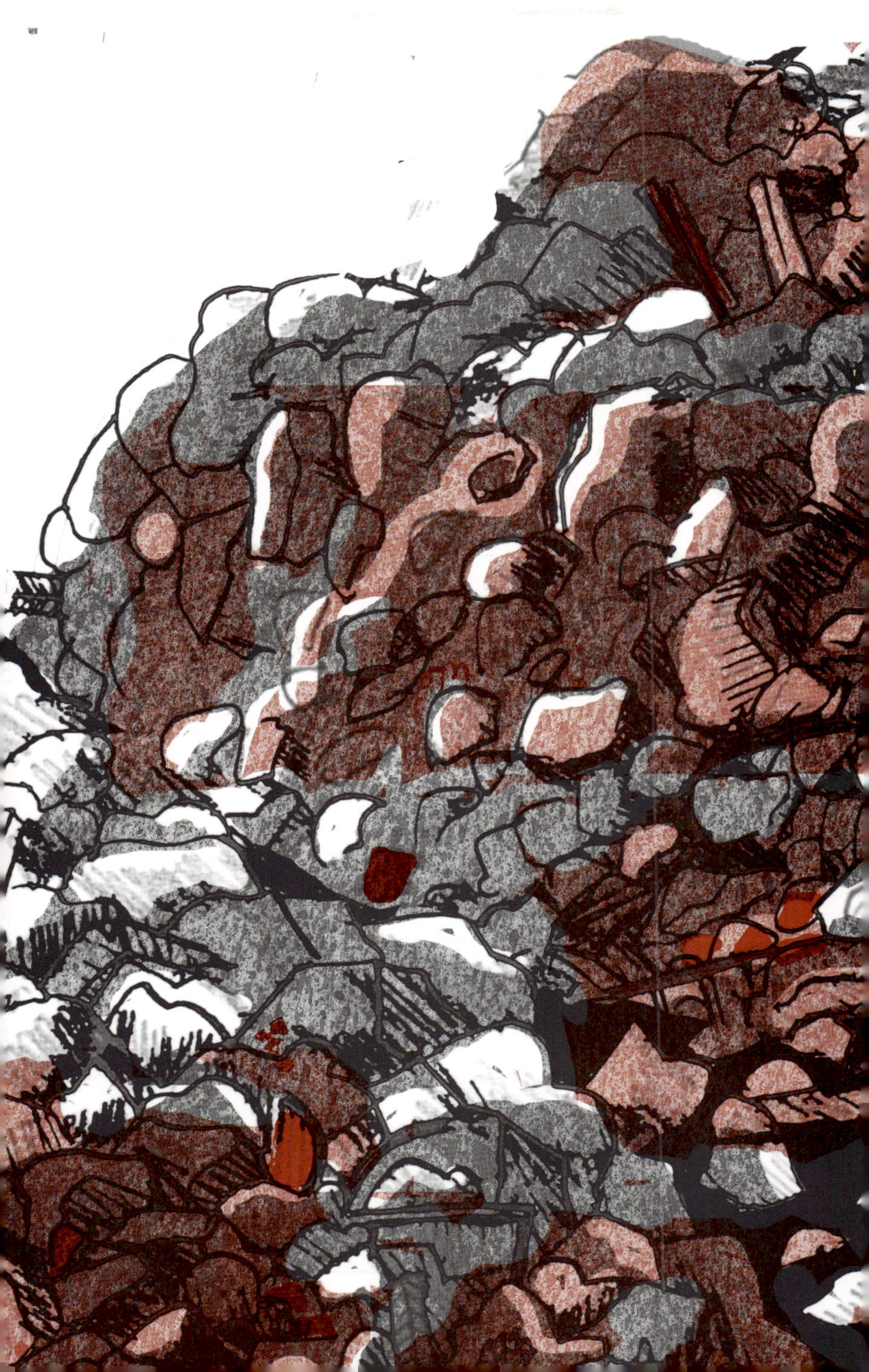

Nek's hands reach out to touch . . .

Memories, stories.

Fragments of lives lived.

Nek looks at these unwanted treasures and thinks of the home he has lost.

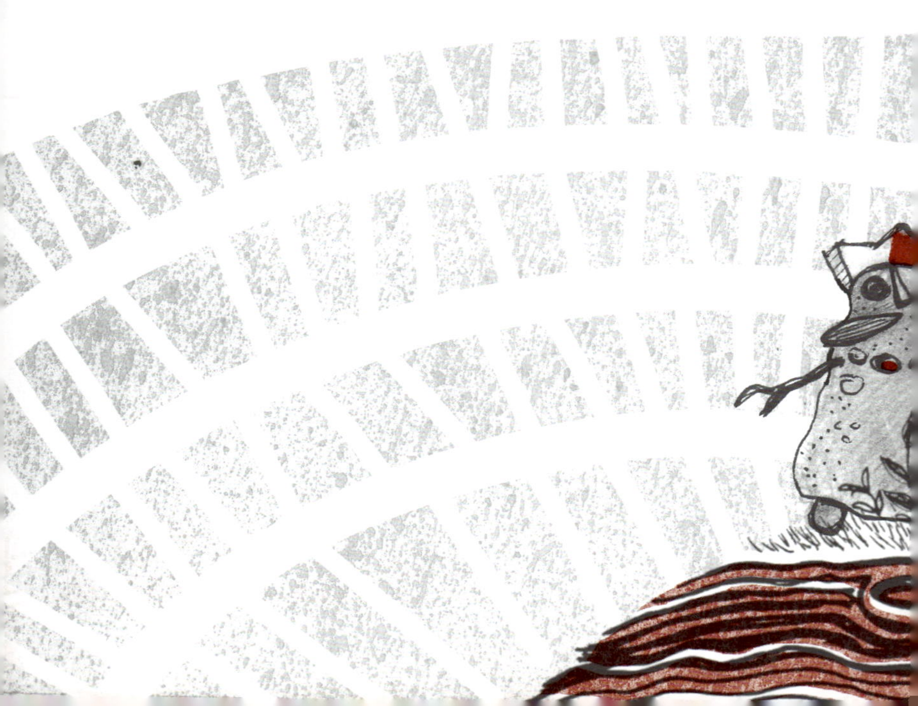

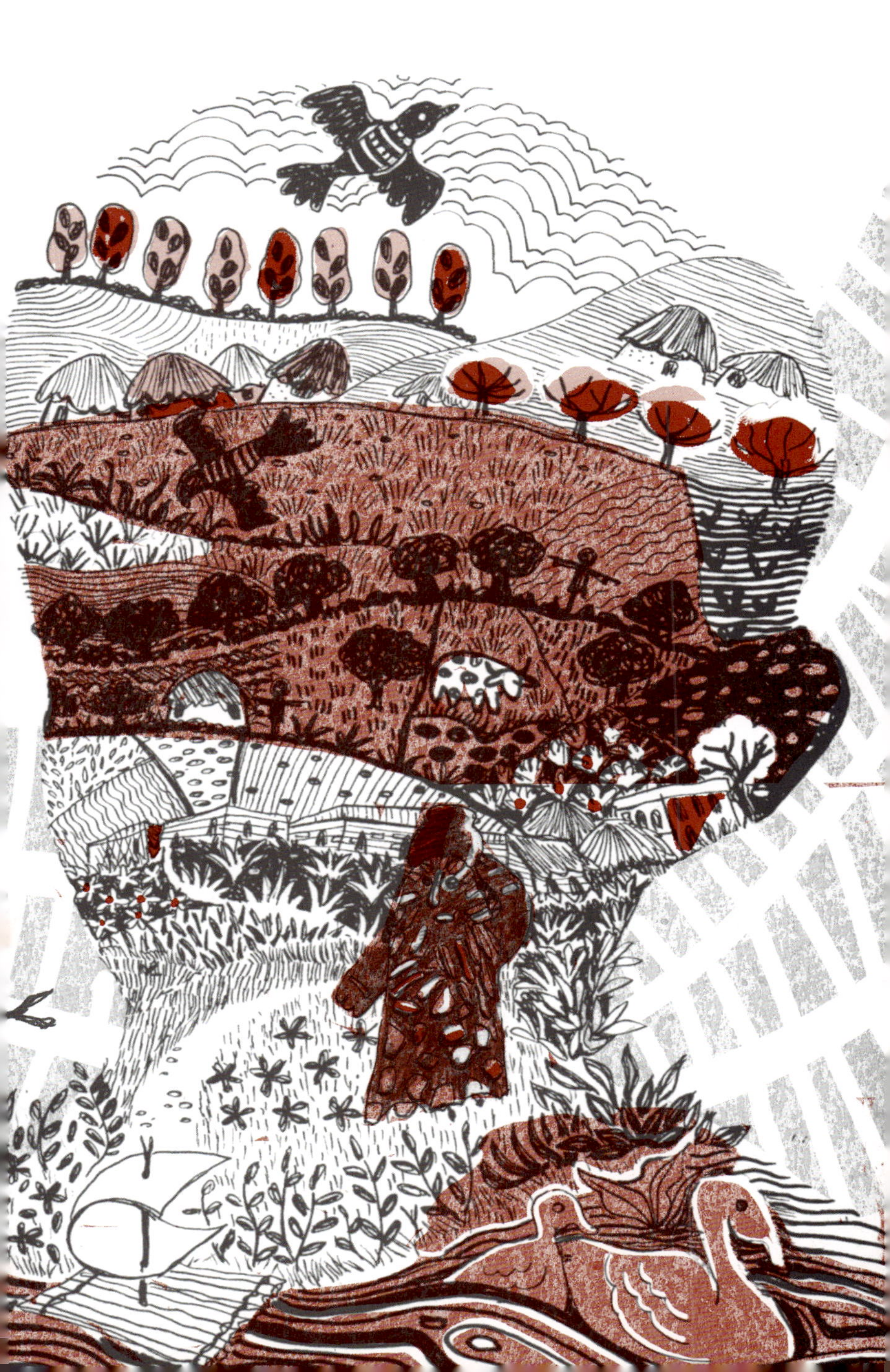

Every day before work, Nek visits the City's waste heaps, collecting its unwanted treasures. On weekends, he cycles to the outskirts to scour the riverbeds for rocks and pebbles.

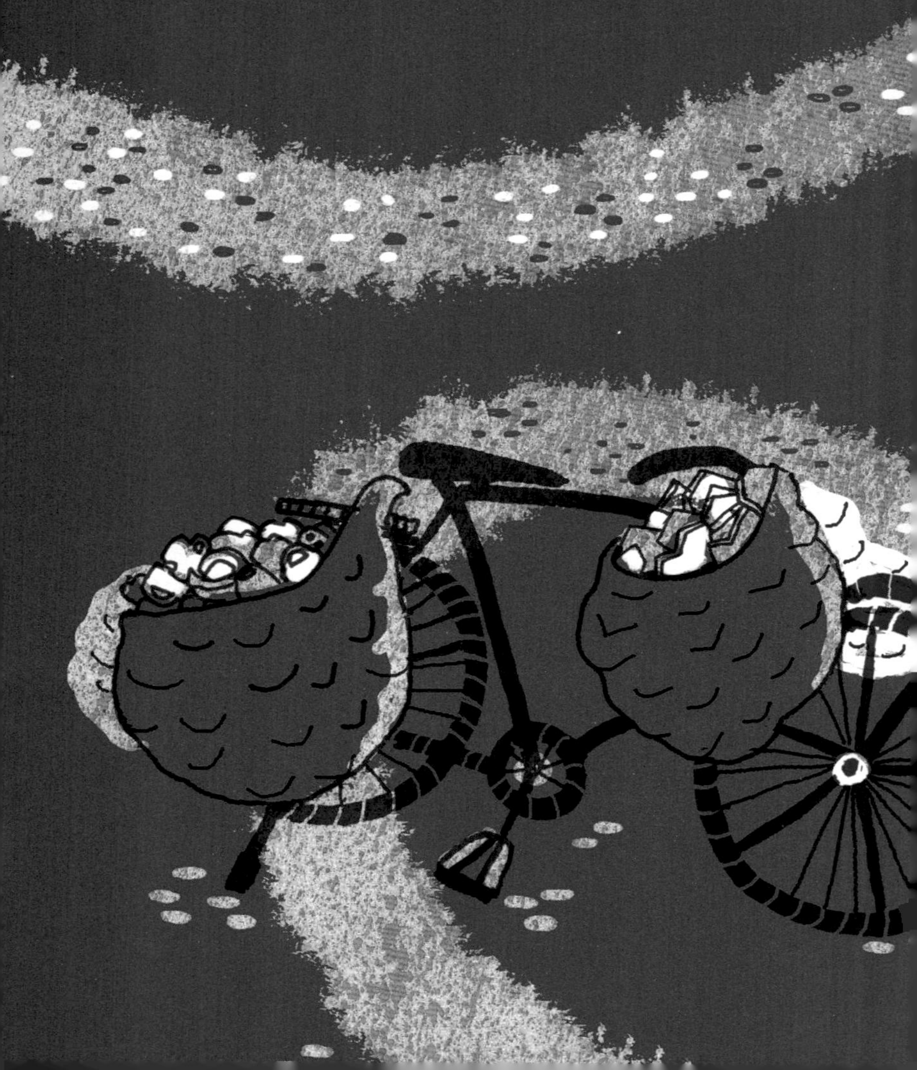

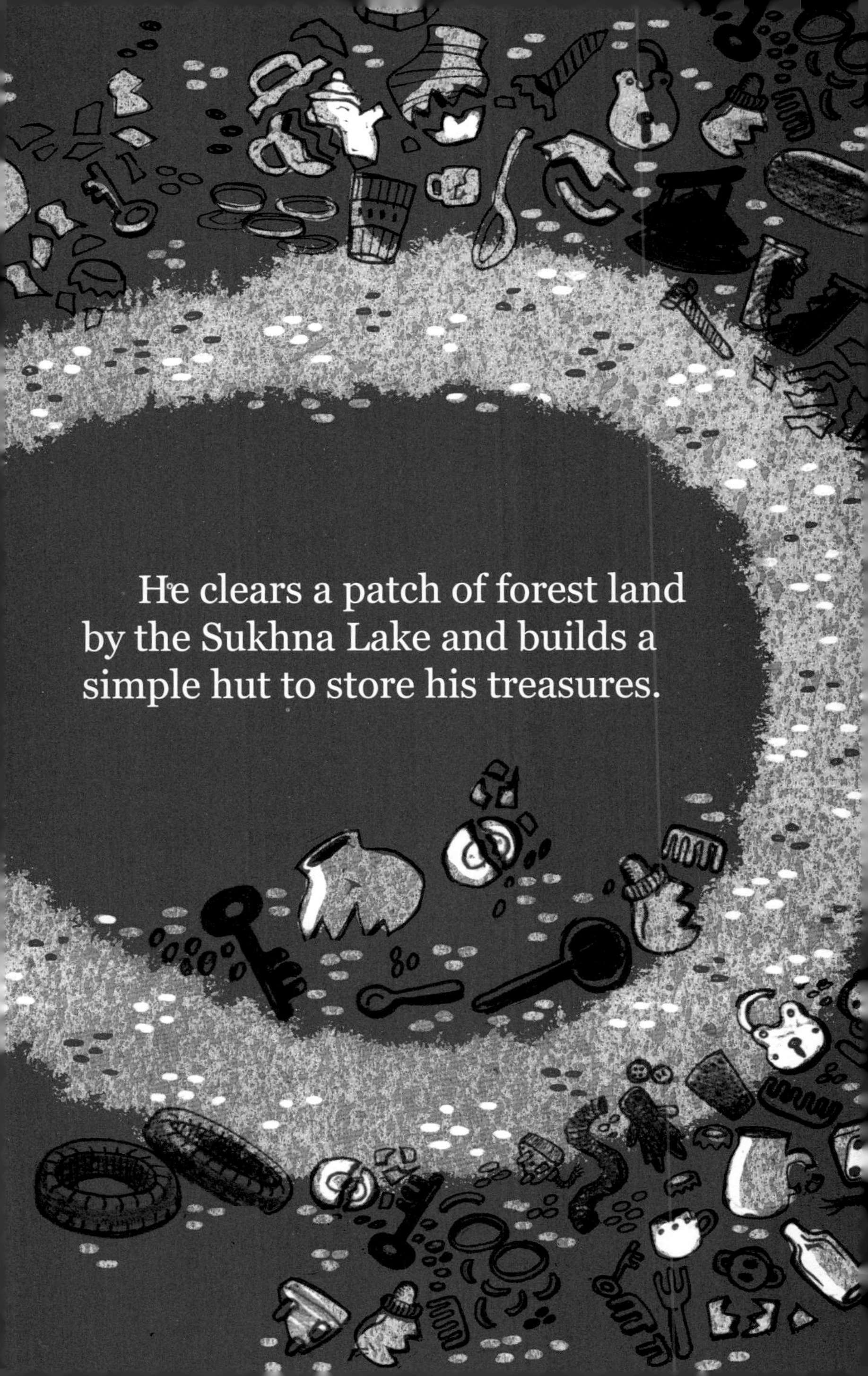

He clears a patch of forest land by the Sukhna Lake and builds a simple hut to store his treasures.

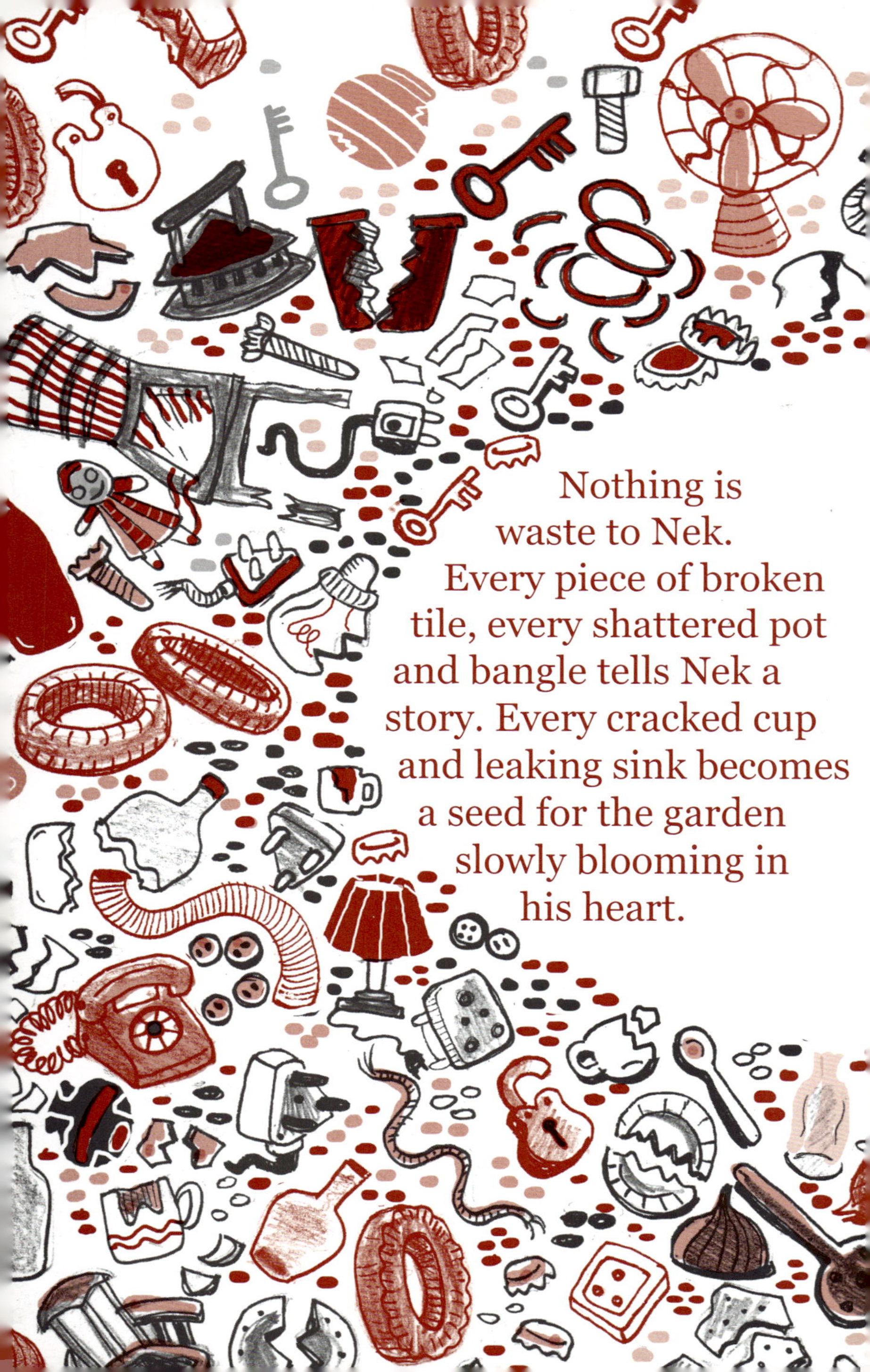

Nothing is
waste to Nek.
Every piece of broken
tile, every shattered pot
and bangle tells Nek a
story. Every cracked cup
and leaking sink becomes
a seed for the garden
slowly blooming in
his heart.

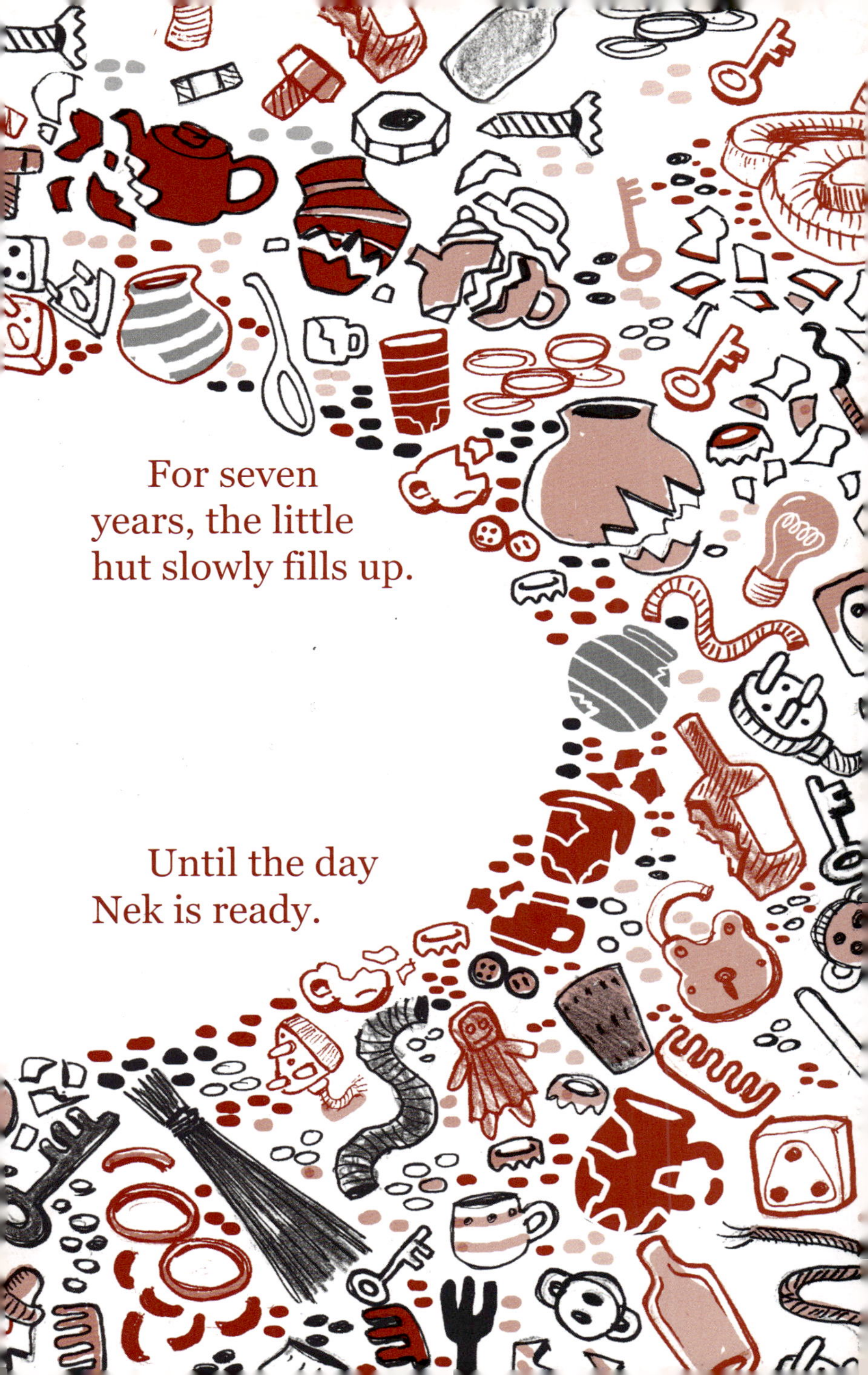
For seven
years, the little
hut slowly fills up.

Until the day
Nek is ready.

He picks up a tile, a piece of bangle. He sees a goddess, a village, a home.

And in that moment, he becomes a boy again.

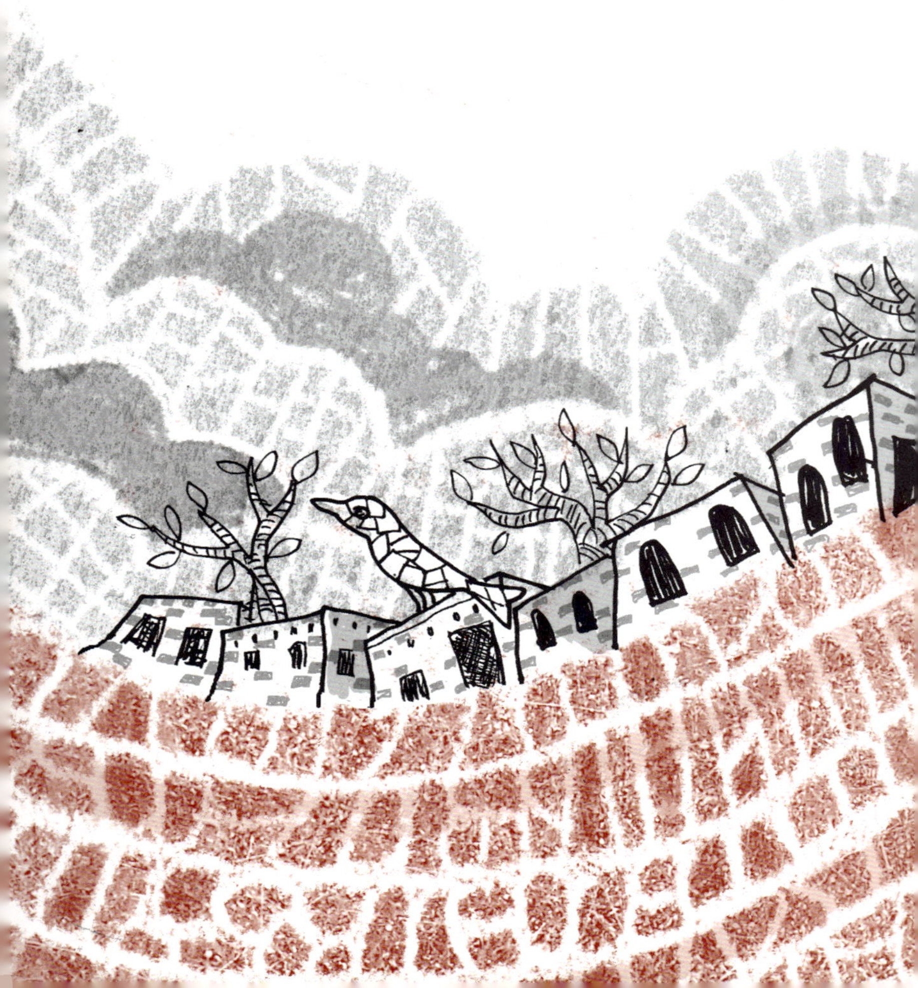

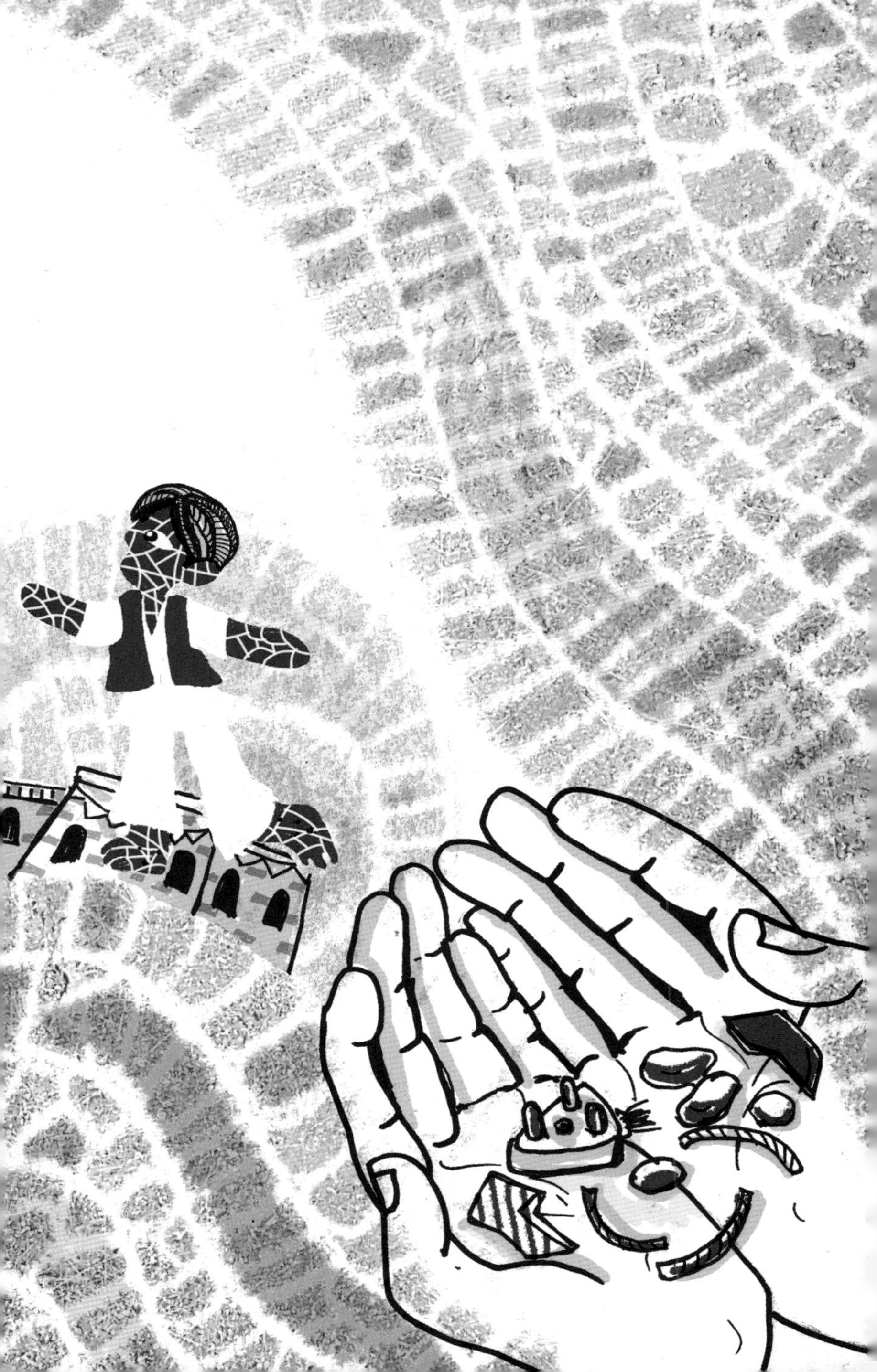

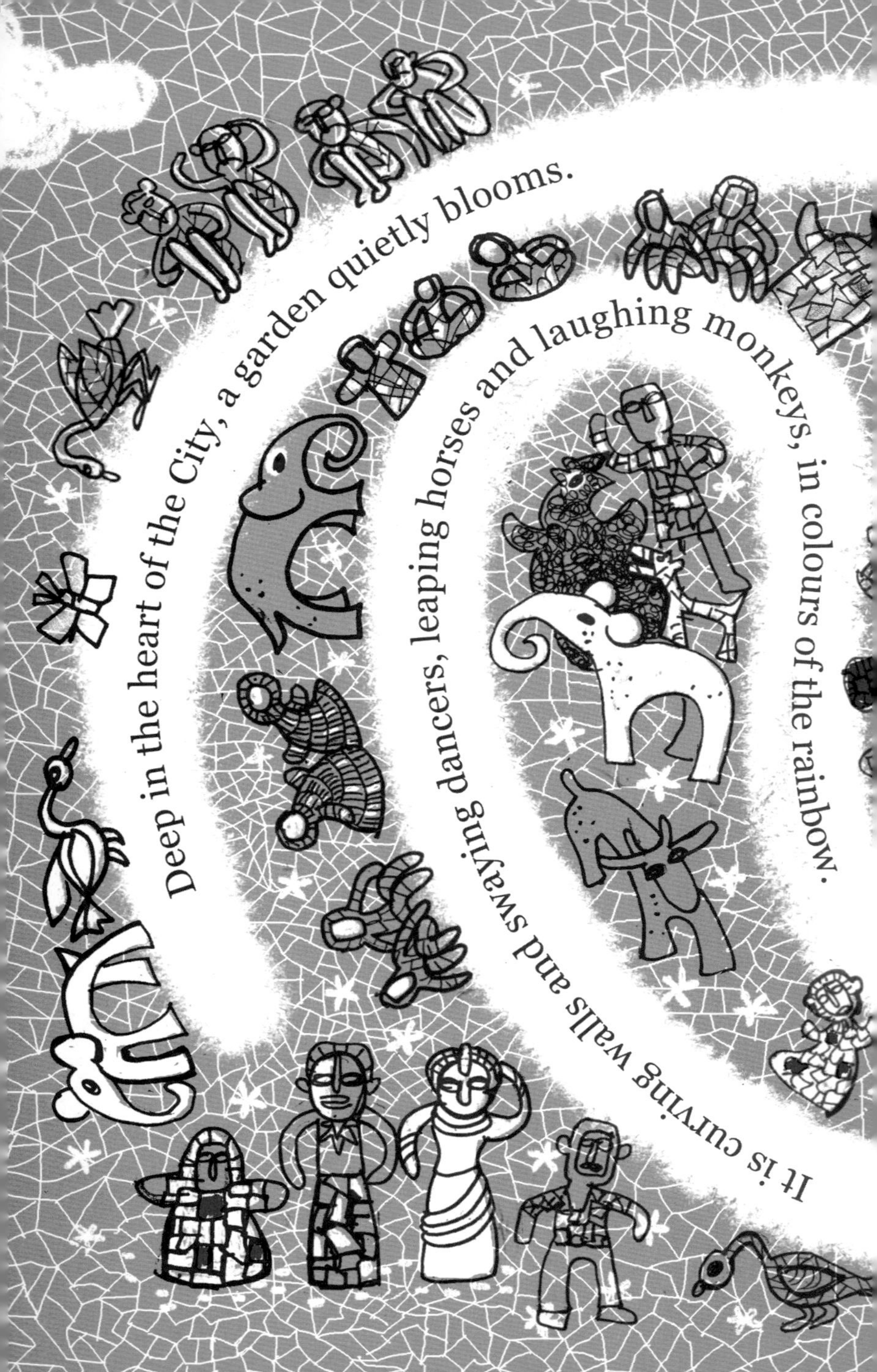
Deep in the heart of the City, a garden quietly blooms.
It is curving walls and swaying dancers, leaping horses and laughing monkeys, in colours of the rainbow.

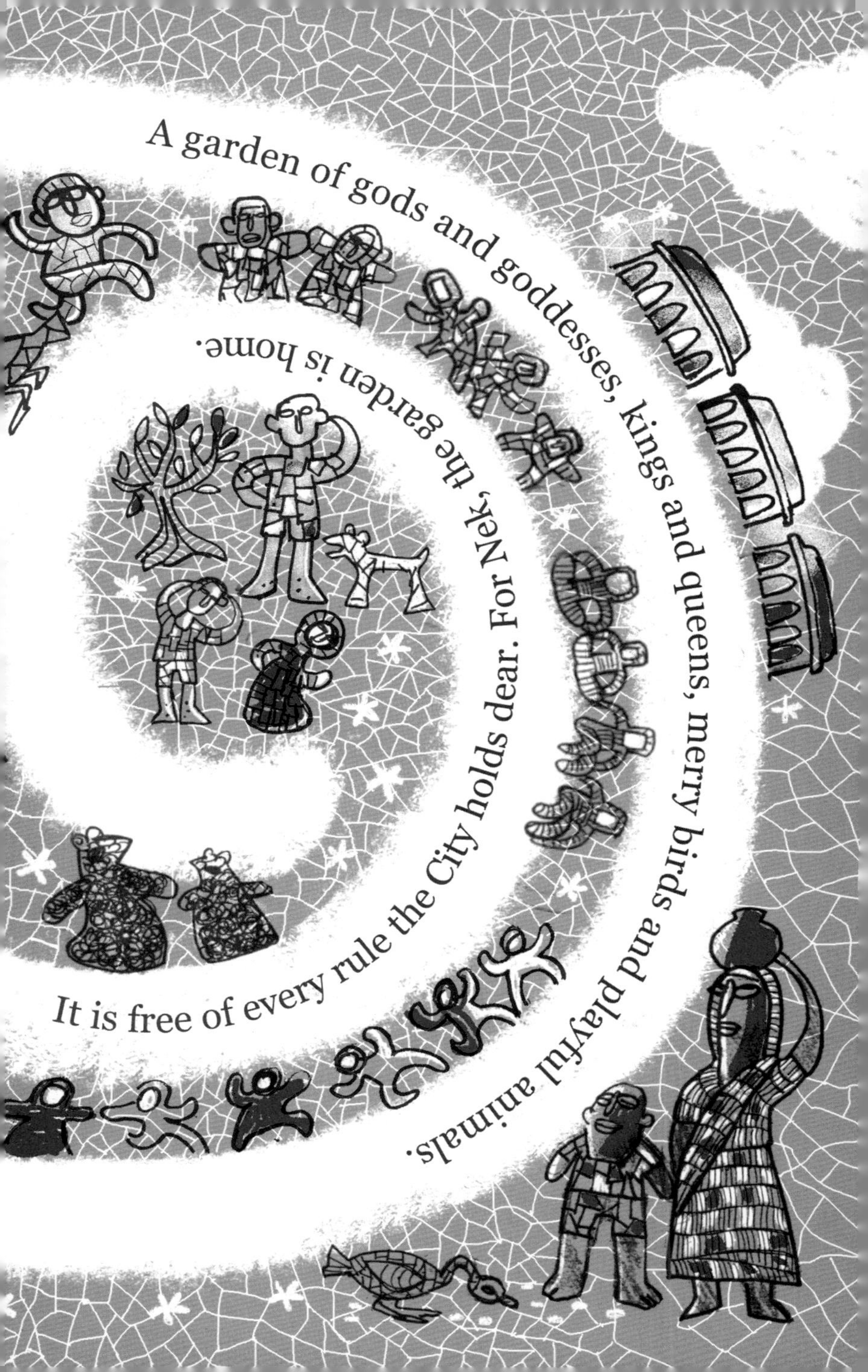

A garden of gods and goddesses, kings and queens, merry birds and playful animals. It is free of every rule the City holds dear. For Nek, the garden is home.

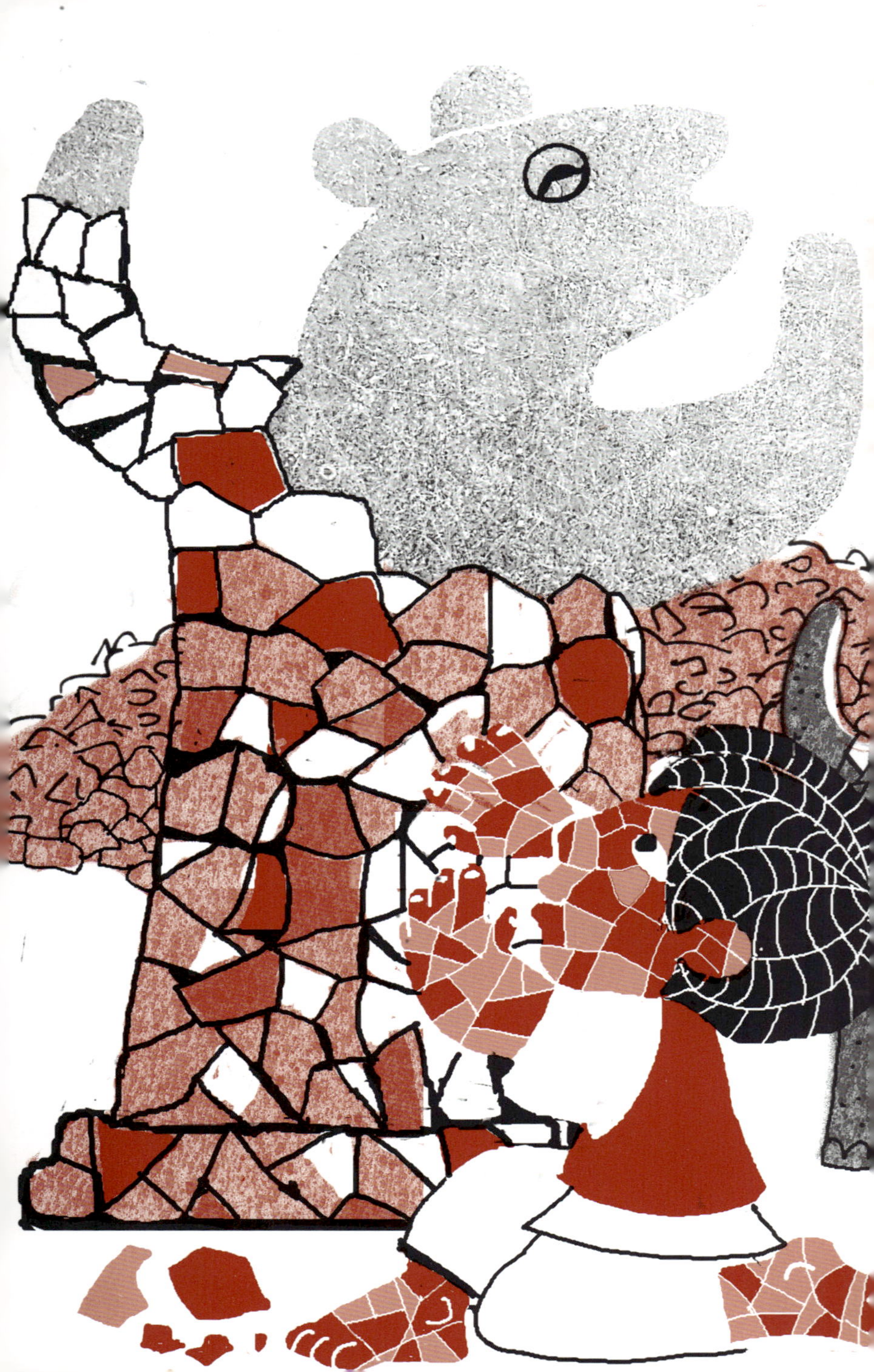

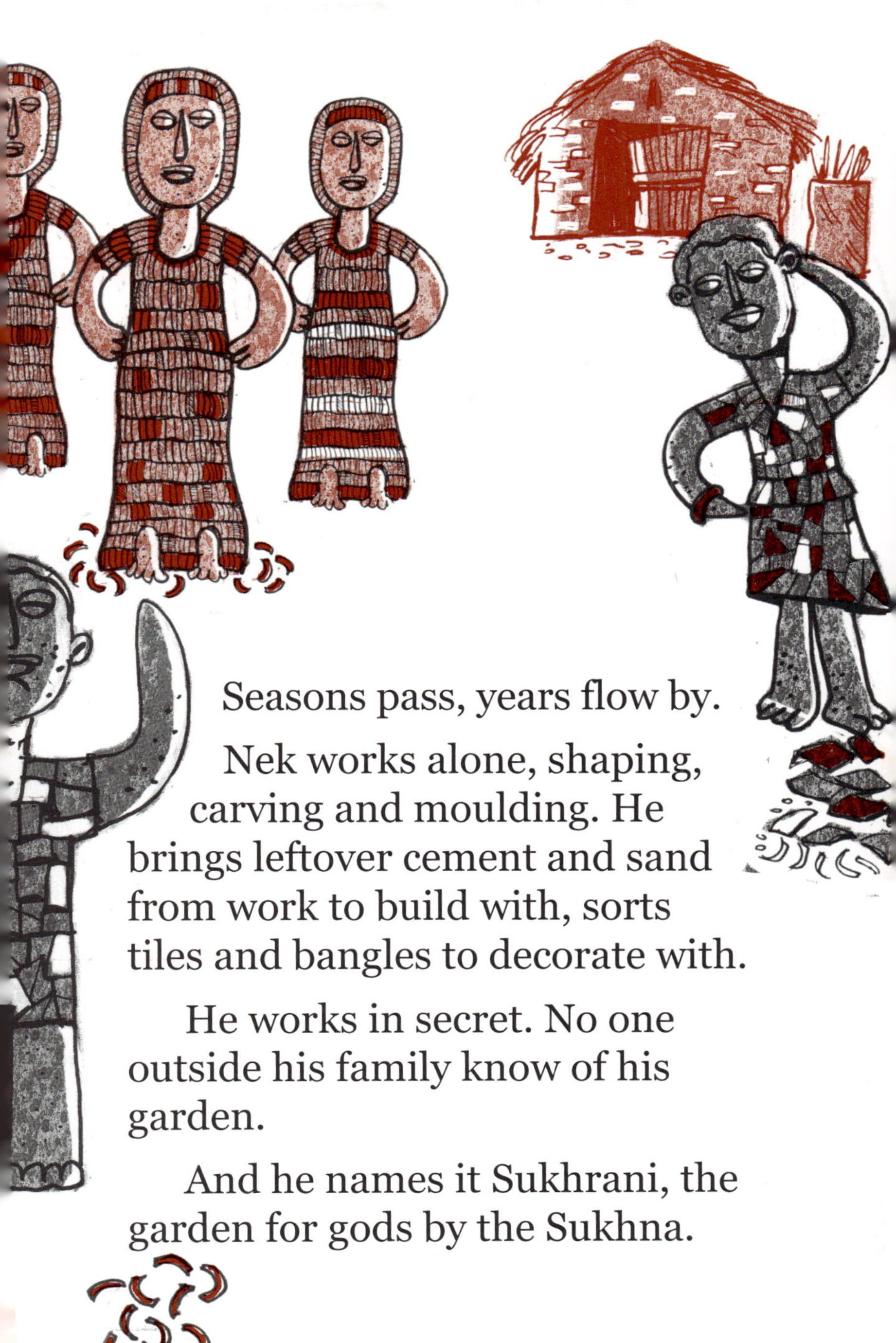

Seasons pass, years flow by.

Nek works alone, shaping, carving and moulding. He brings leftover cement and sand from work to build with, sorts tiles and bangles to decorate with.

He works in secret. No one outside his family know of his garden.

And he names it Sukhrani, the garden for gods by the Sukhna.

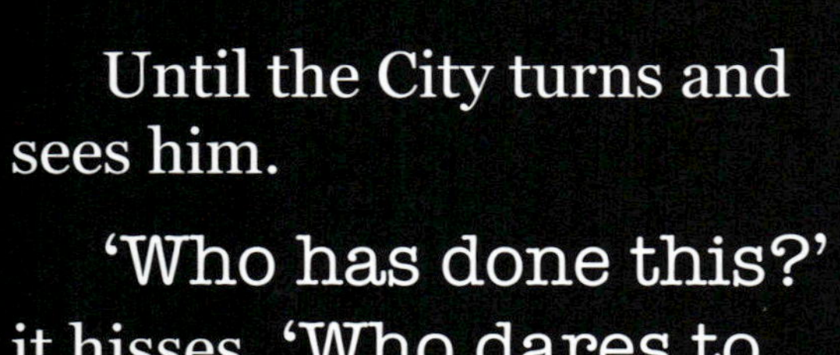

Until the City turns and sees him.

'Who has done this?' it hisses. 'Who dares to break my rules and disrupt my order?'

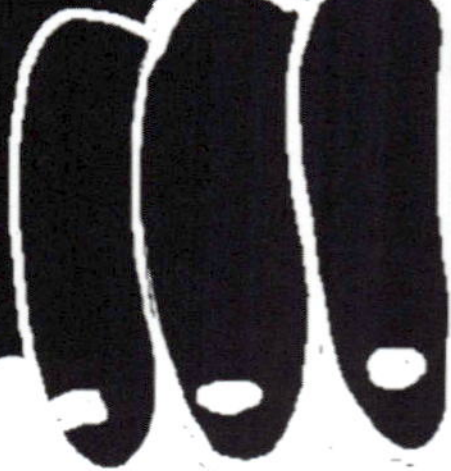

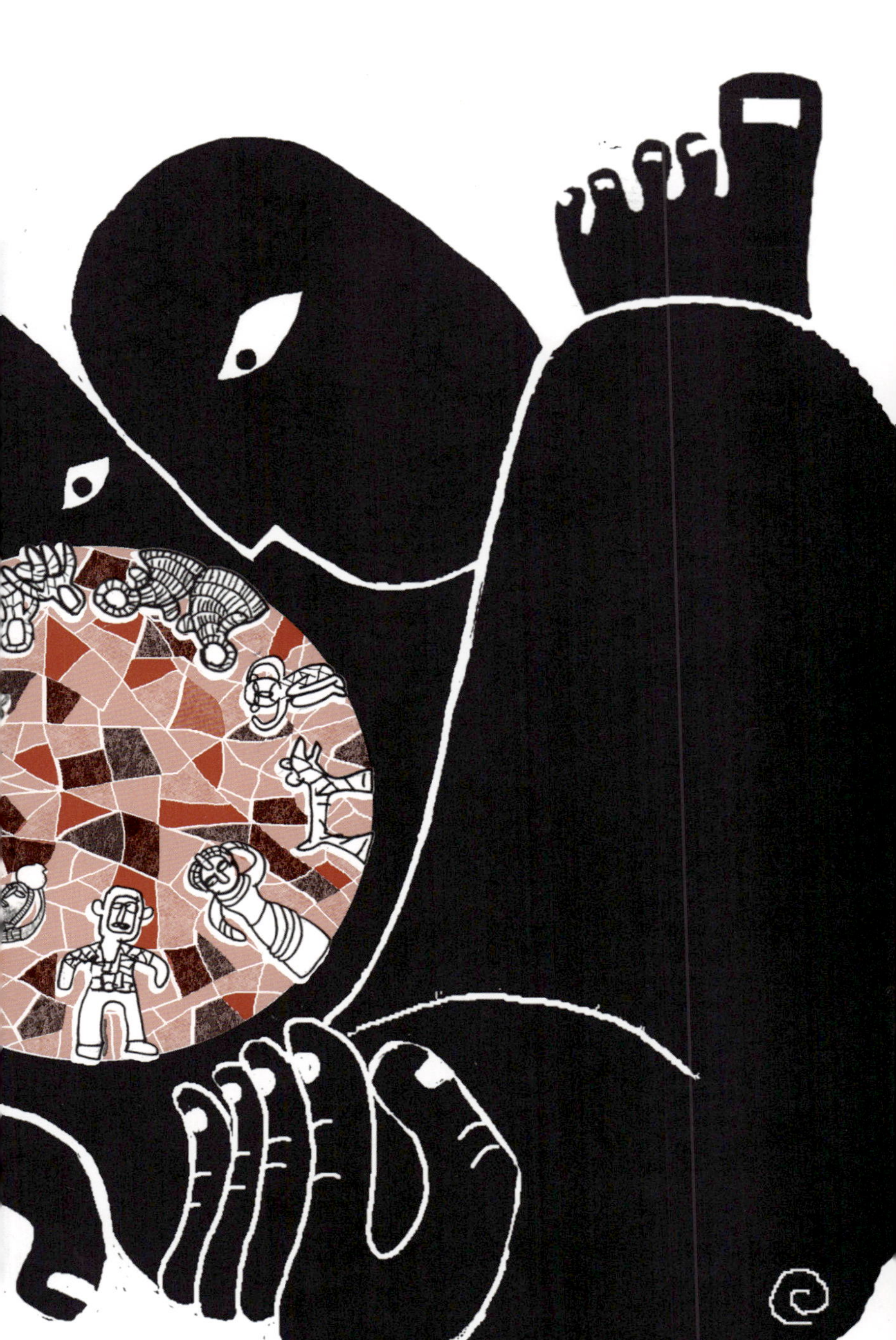

'A garden grows to its own rules,' says Nek.

'It disobeys mine!' the City rages. 'It steals from me!'

'But these were things you threw away,' says Nek. 'And this is land you were never going to use.'

The City rages in fury. It wants to destroy Sukhrani!

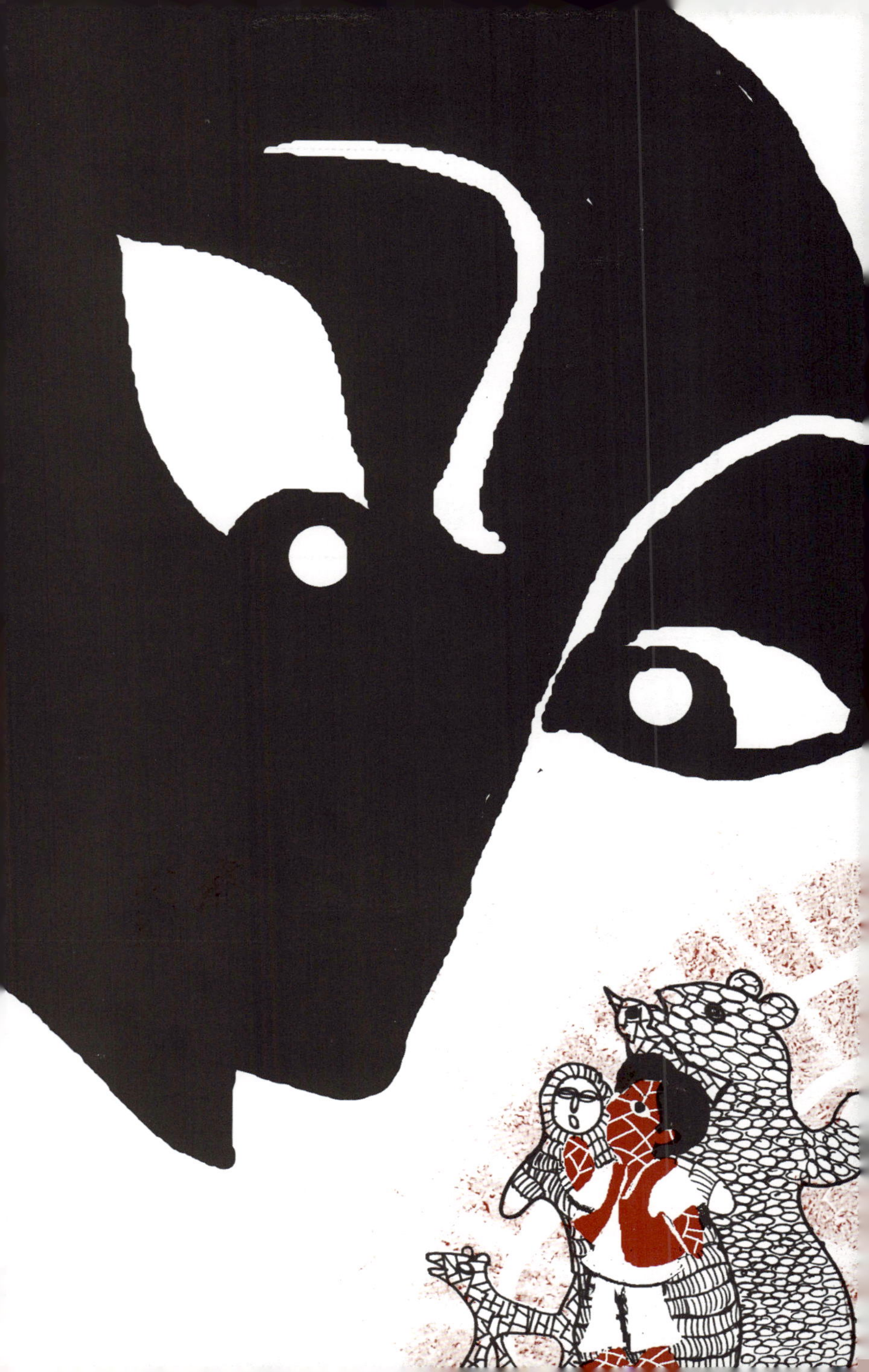

But as the City rages, its people are drawn to the garden. *Has it really defied the City*, they wonder. *Has it dared to break its rules?*

One by one, they step into Nek's garden.

They wander through its curving pathways, reaching out to touch its smooth surfaces.

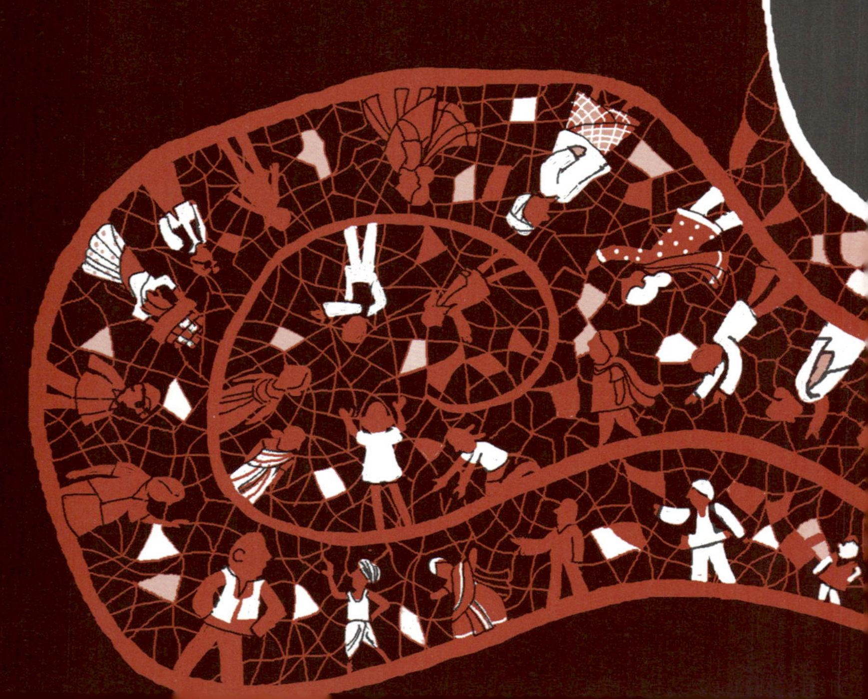

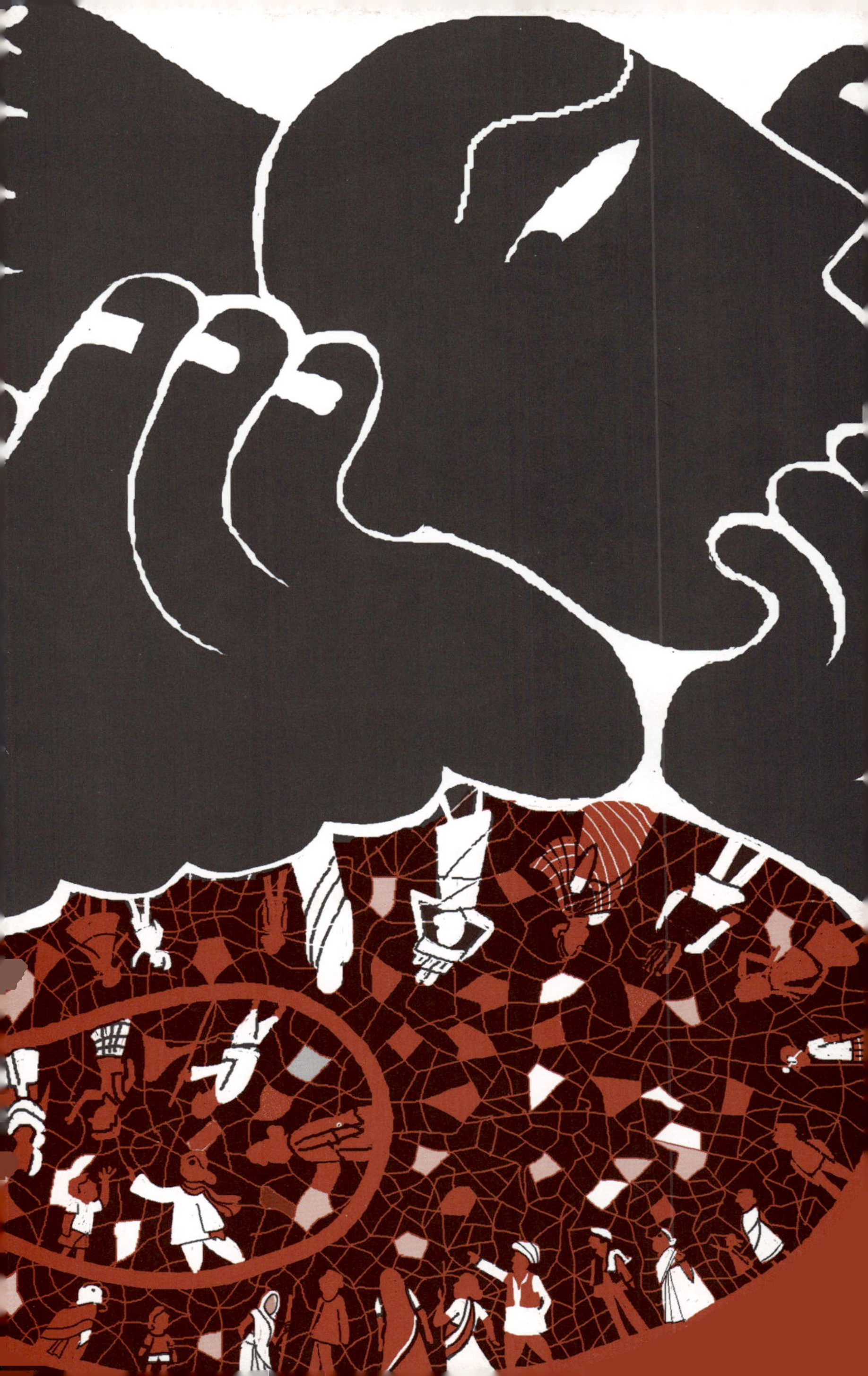

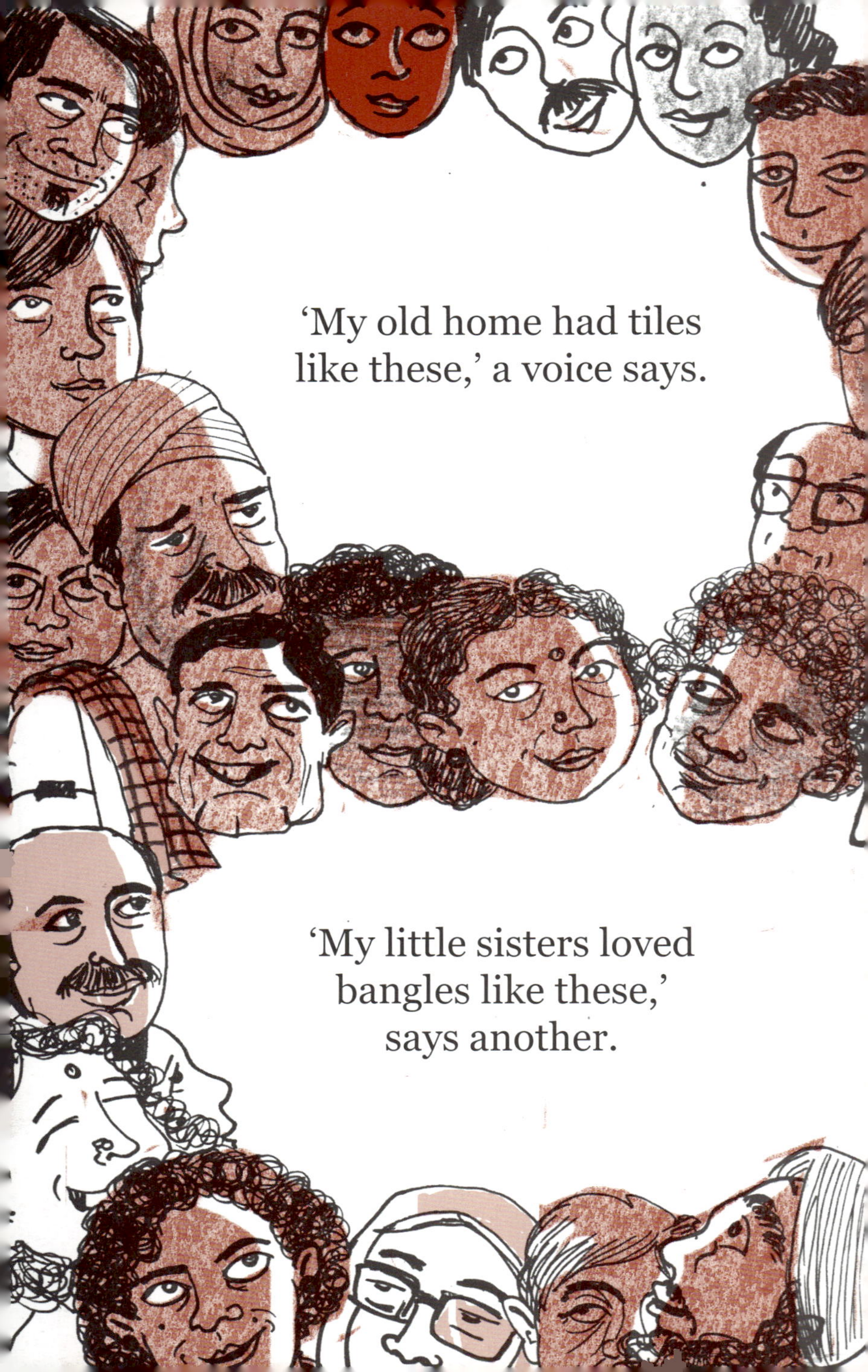
'My old home had tiles
like these,' a voice says.
'My little sisters loved
bangles like these,'
says another.

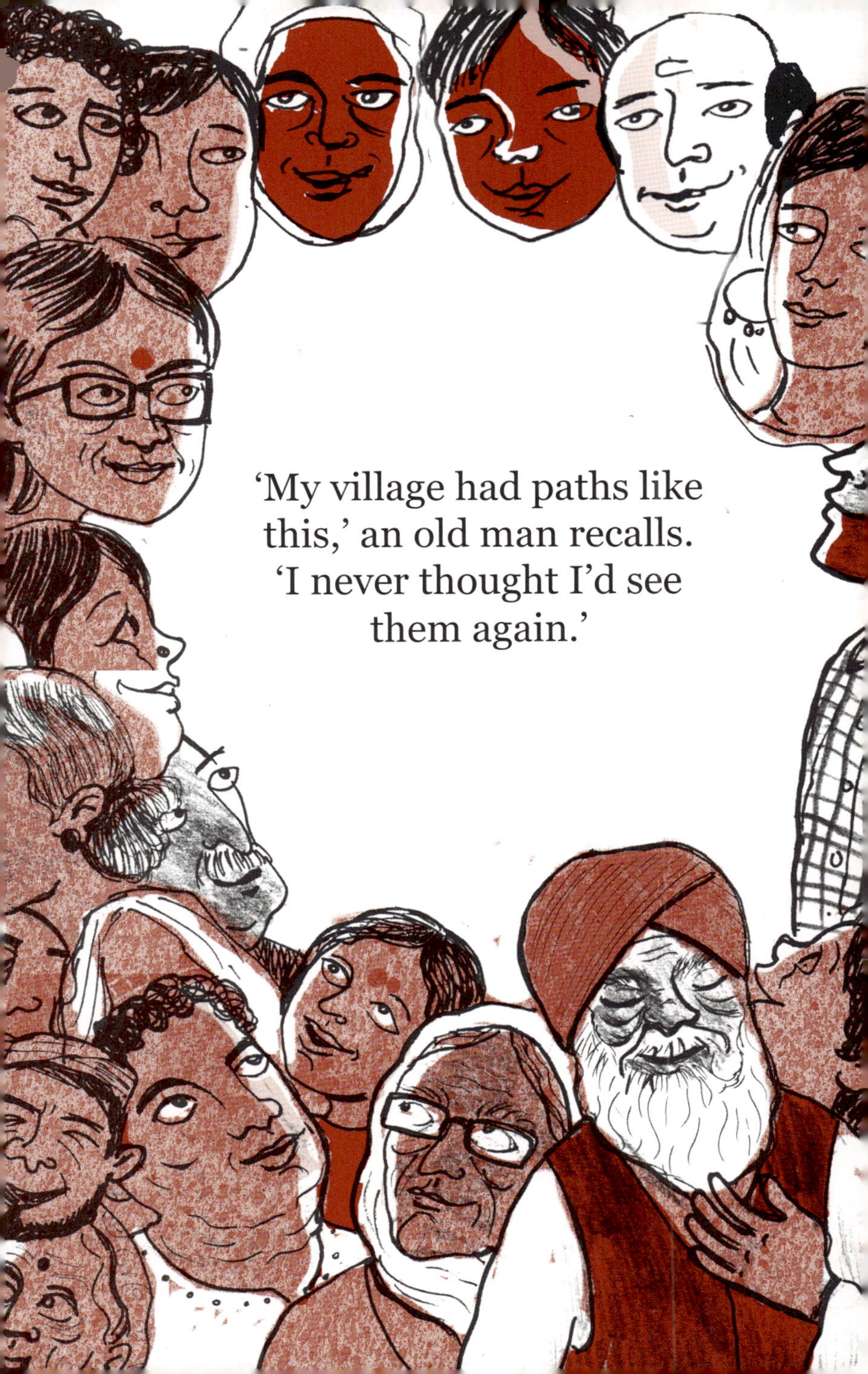

'My village had paths like this,' an old man recalls. 'I never thought I'd see them again.'

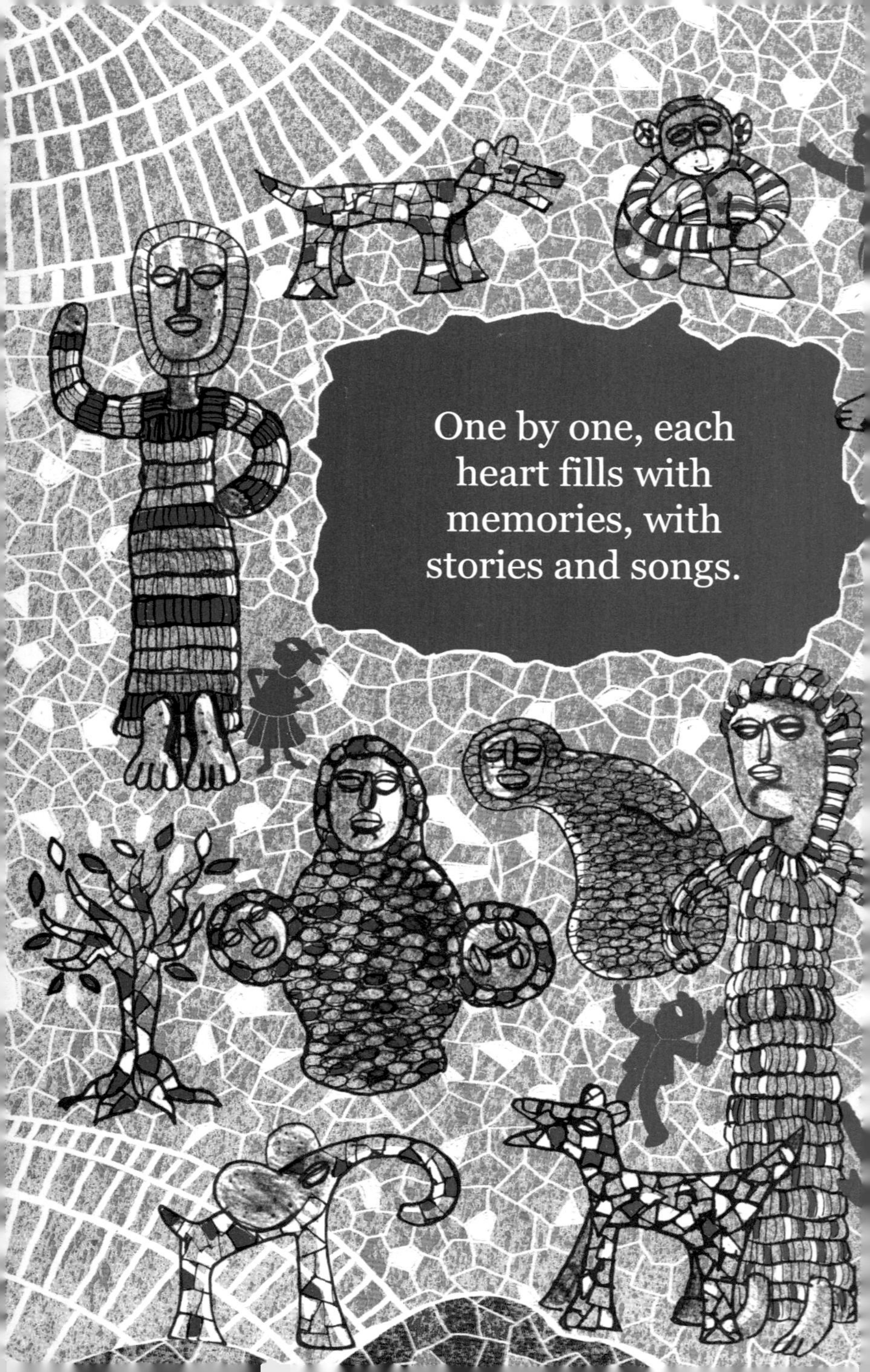
One by one, each heart fills with memories, with stories and songs.

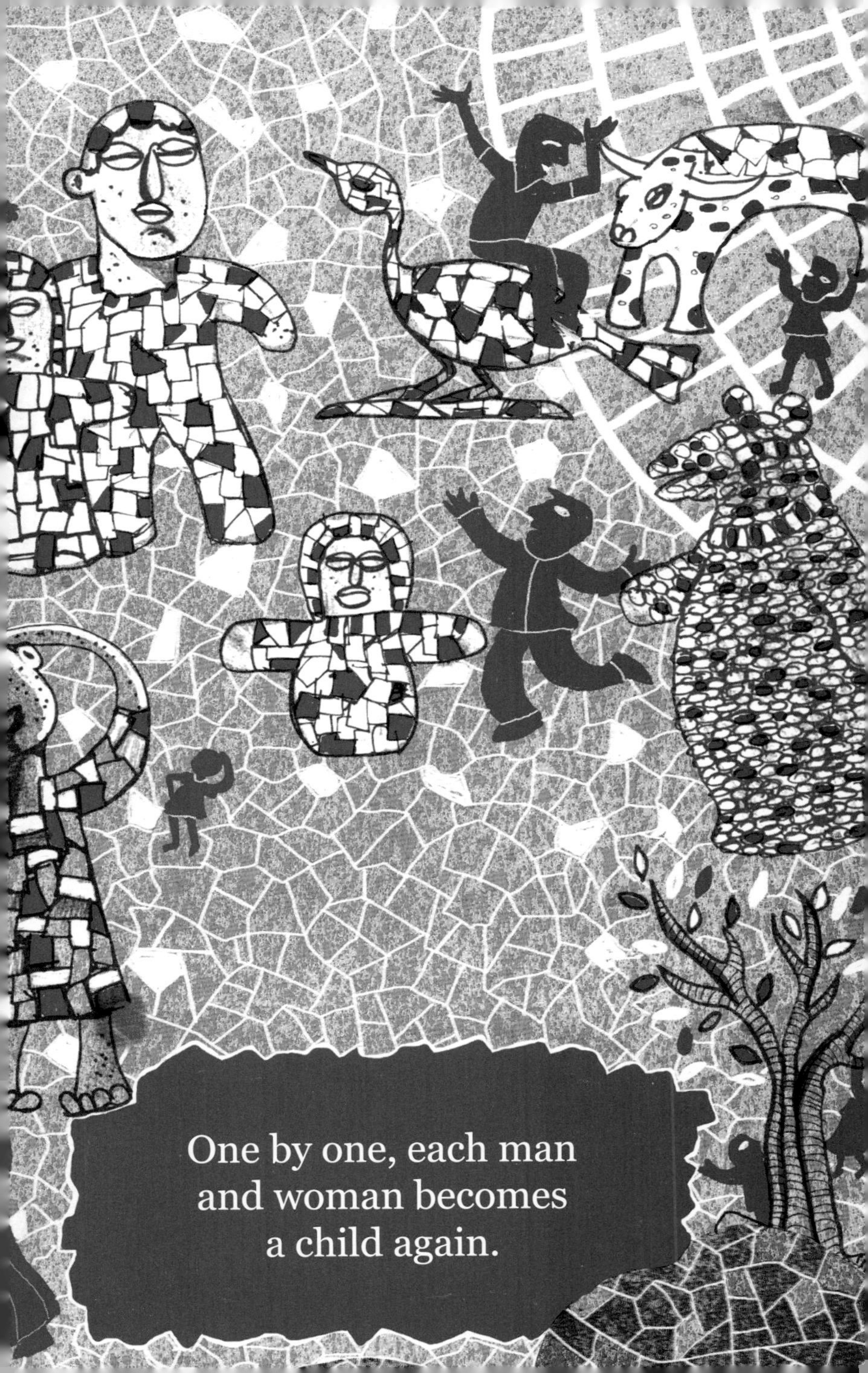
One by one, each man
and woman becomes
a child again.

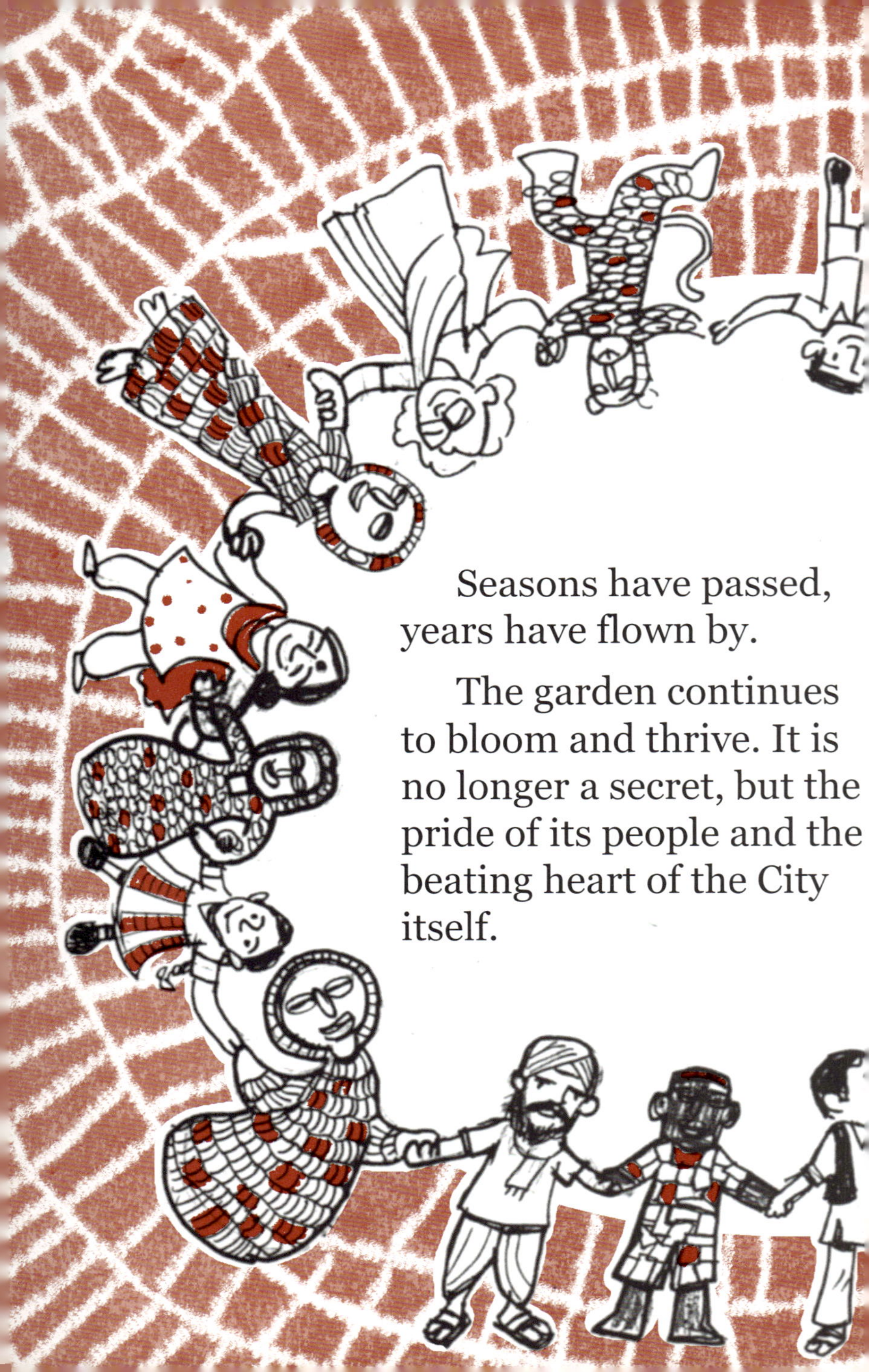

Seasons have passed, years have flown by.

The garden continues to bloom and thrive. It is no longer a secret, but the pride of its people and the beating heart of the City itself.

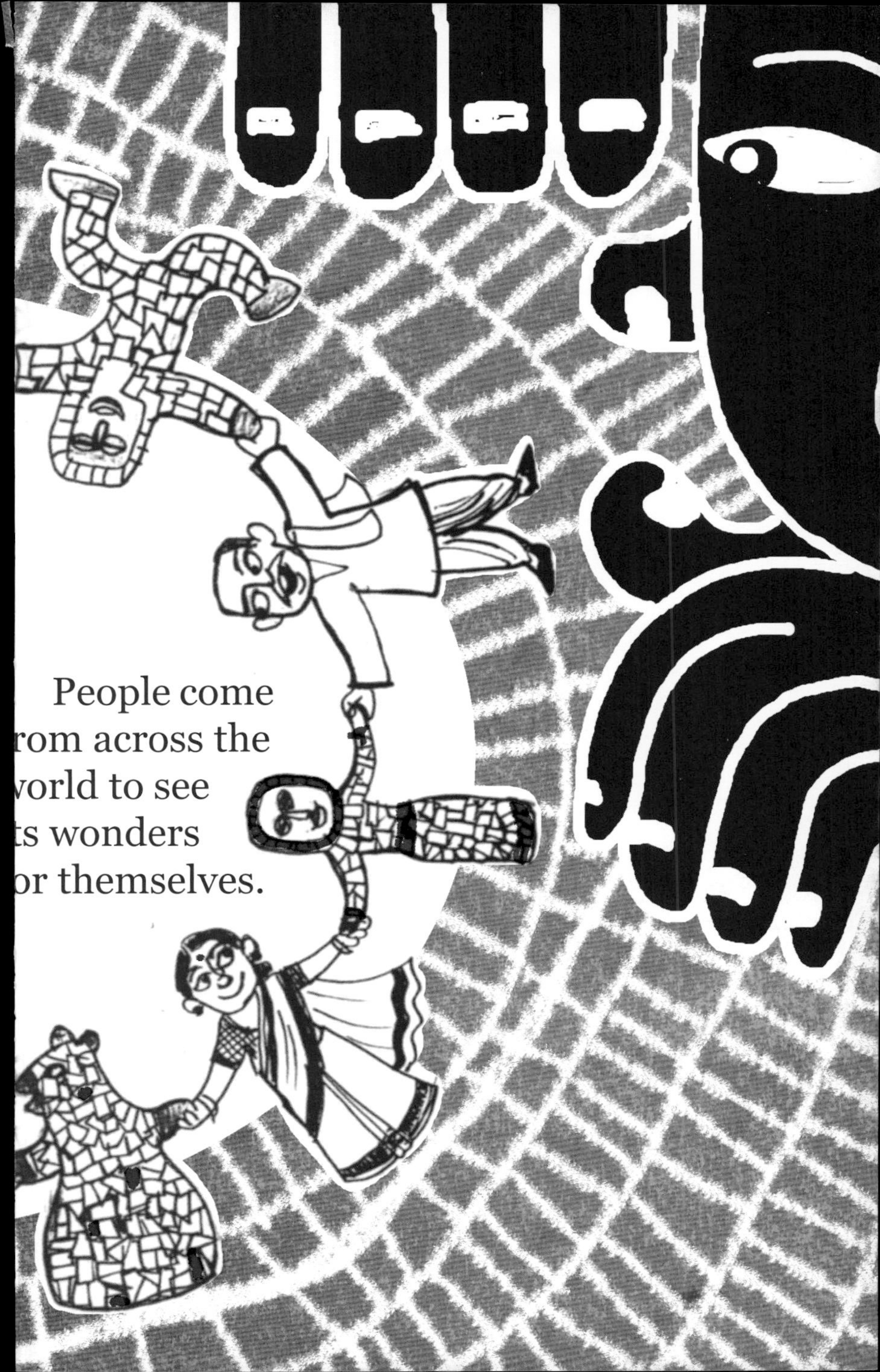
People come
from across the
world to see
its wonders
for themselves.

And every heart is touched by the magic of Sukhrani.

Nek Chand's garden takes you back home.

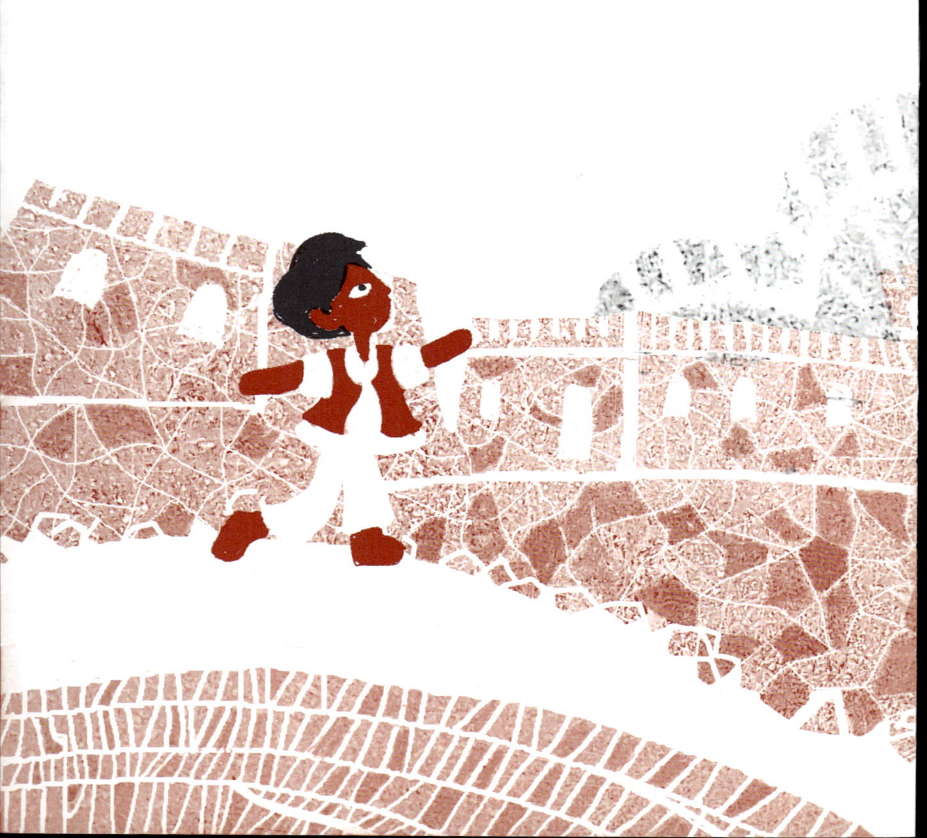

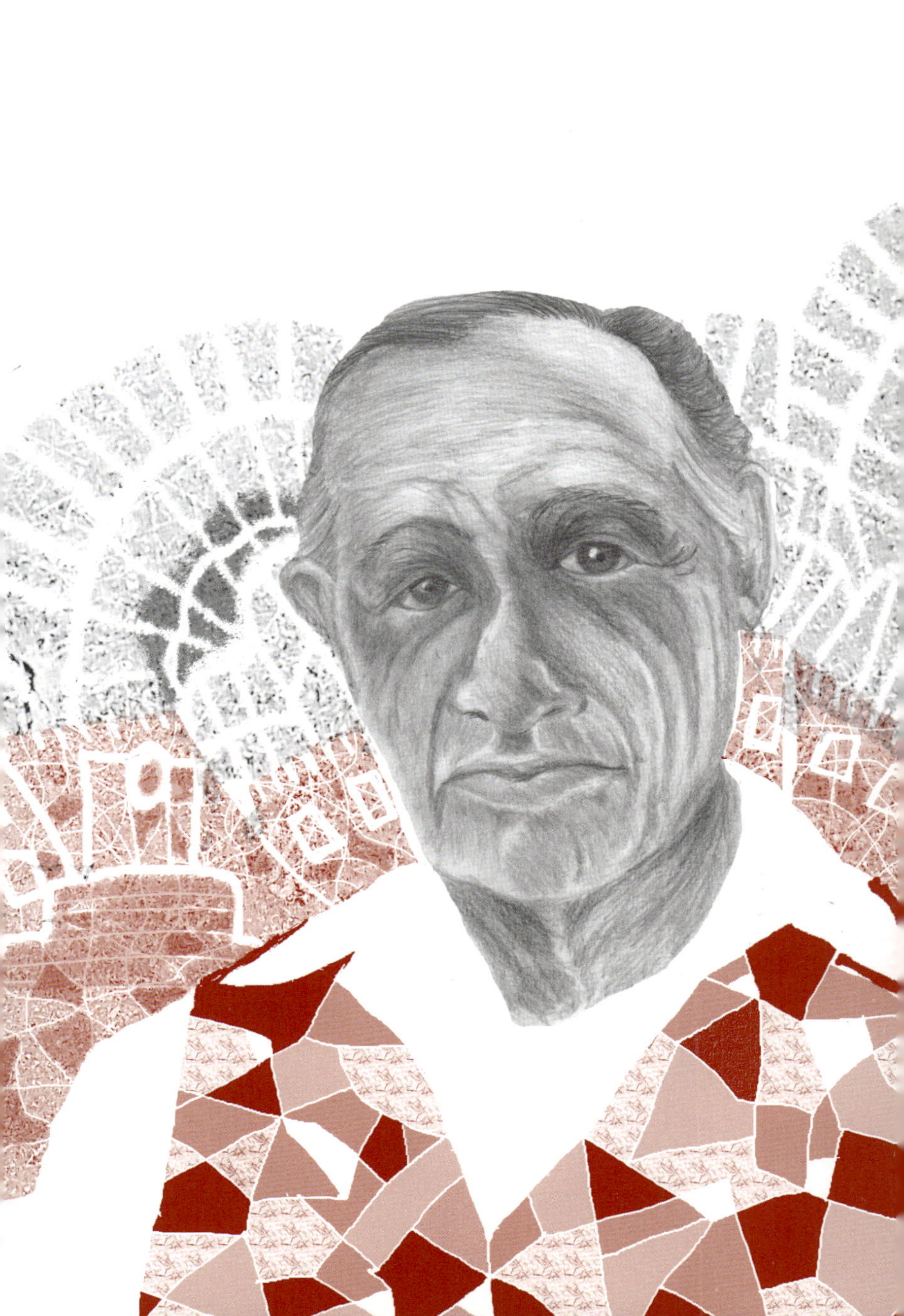

Chandigarh was the first planned city in independent India. It was designed by the legendary architect Le Corbusier to reflect modern ideas and lifestyles. His plans for the city did not allow for any gardens or sculptures other than the ones he had designed.

Nek Chand Saini (15 December 1924— 12 June 2015) dedicated his life to building Sukhrani. When city authorities discovered it, he had already been working on it for eighteen years, and it covered thirteen acres. It was almost demolished, before the people of Chandigarh stepped up to protect it. Today, the garden spans over forty acres and is visited by thousands of people every day.

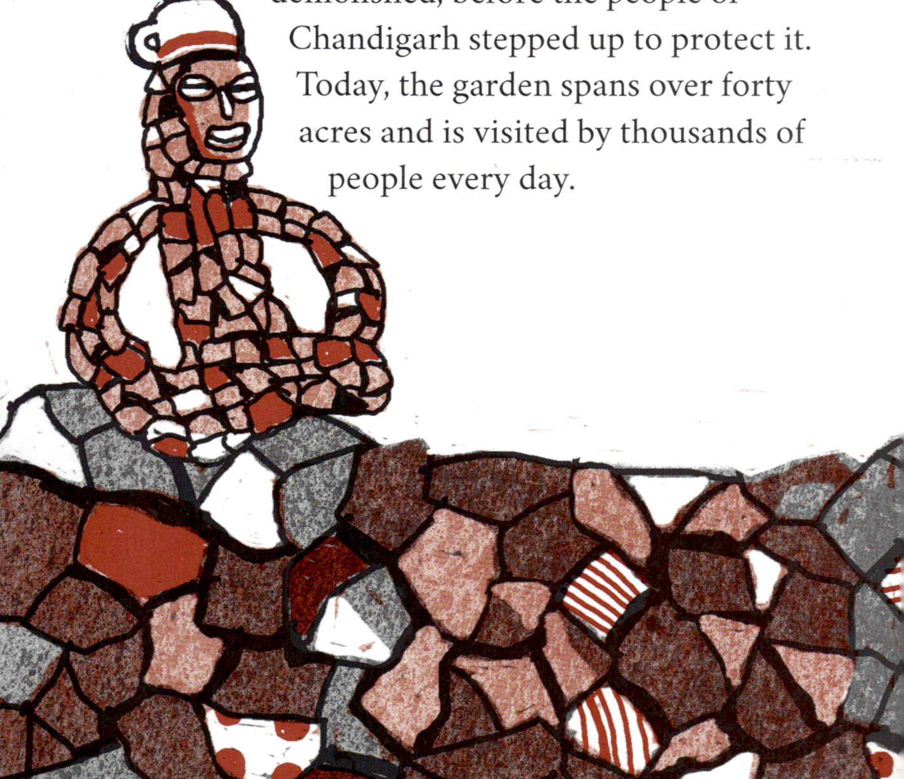

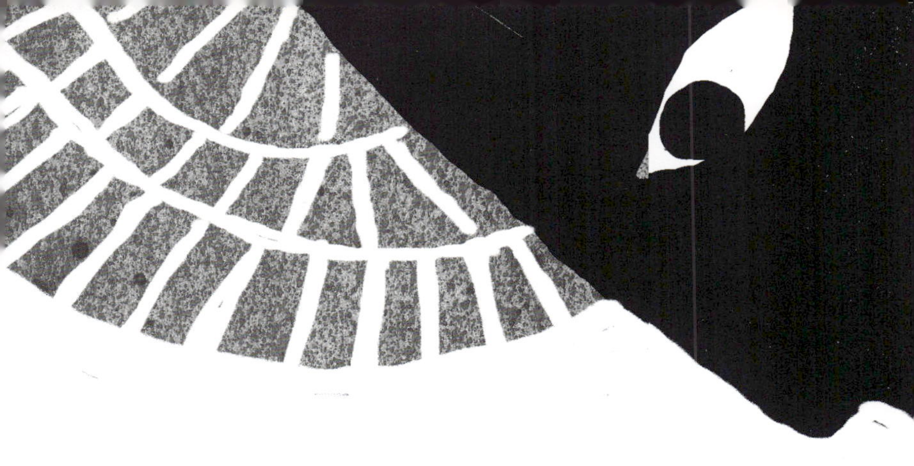

Nek Chand Saini was awarded a Padma Shri
for his unique work. He travelled the world,
giving lectures on his art.

*The illustrations in this book are inspired by
Nek Chand's sculptures and the architecture of
Chandigarh.*

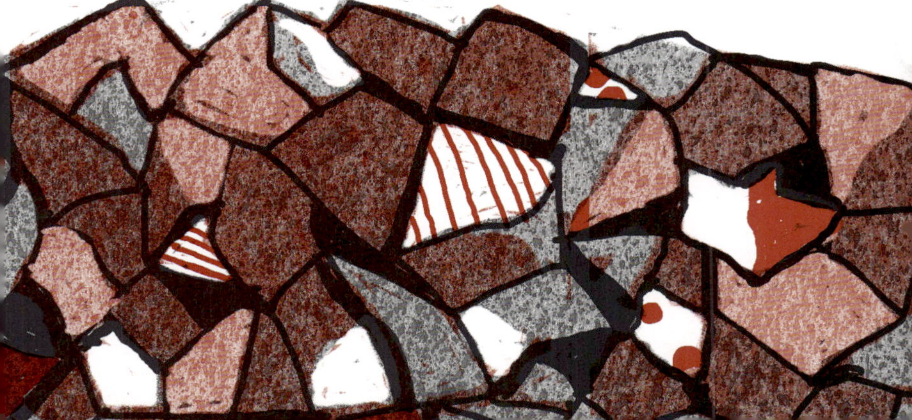

Lavanya Karthik is an author and illustrator by day, a cookie monster by teatime and fast asleep by nine at night. She lives in Mumbai where she eats a lot of chocolate and takes a lot of naps.

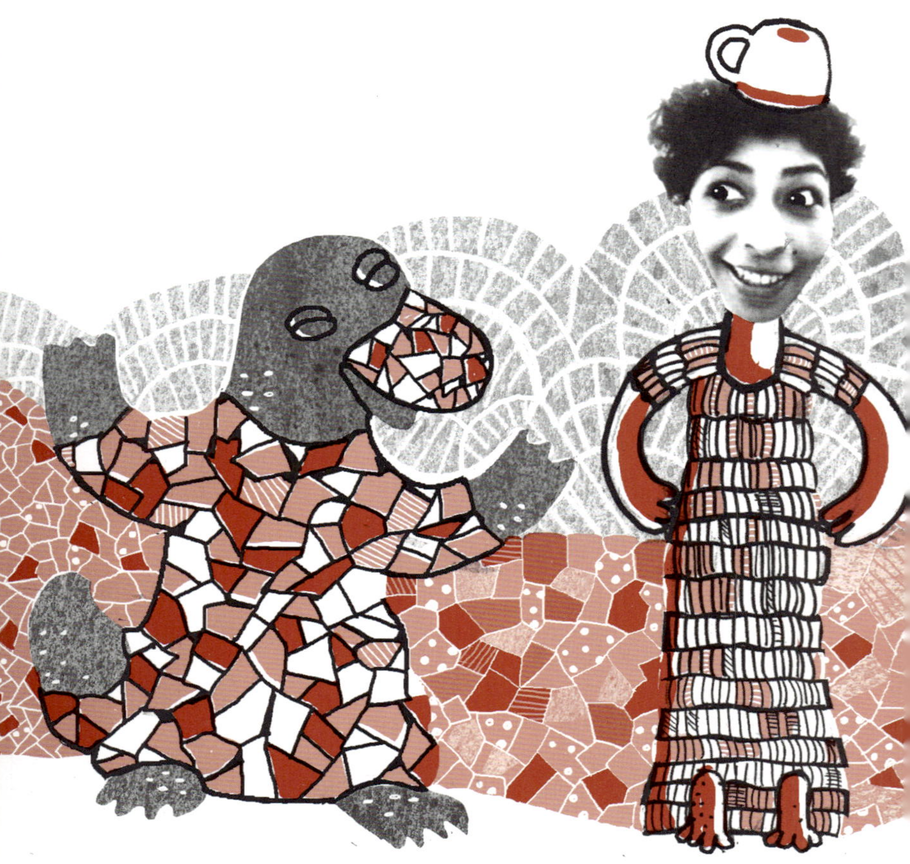